The Fire Within

By Patricia Wentworth

A Digireads.com Book
Digireads.com Publishing
16212 Riggs Rd
Stilwell, KS, 66085

The Fire Within
By Patricia Wentworth
ISBN: 1-4209-2903-8

Please visit *www.digireads.com*

CHAPTER I

MR. MOTTISFONT'S OPINION OF HIS NEPHEW

As I was going adown the dale
　Sing derry down dale, and derry down dale,
　As I was going adown the dale,
　Adown the dale of a Monday,
With never a thought of the Devil his tricks,
Why who should I meet with his bundle of sticks,
But the very old man of the Nursery tale,
　Sing derry down dale, and derry down dale,
The wicked old man of the Nursery tale
　Who gathered his sticks of a Sunday.
Sing derry down, derry down dale.

OLD Mr. Edward Mottisfont looked over the edge of the sheet at David Blake.

"My nephew Edward is most undoubtedly and indisputably a prig—a damned prig," he added thoughtfully after a moment's pause for reflection. As he reflected his black eyes danced from David's face to a crayon drawing which hung on the paneled wall above the mantelpiece.

"His mother's fault," he observed, "it's not so bad in a woman, and she was pretty, which Edward ain't. Pretty and a prig my sister Sarah—"

There was a faint emphasis on the word sister, and David remembered having heard his mother say that both Edward and William Mottisfont had been in love with the girl whom William married. "And a plain prig my nephew Edward," continued the old gentleman. "Damn it all, David, why can't I leave my money to you instead?"

"Because I shouldn't take it, sir," he said.

He was sitting, most unprofessionally, on the edge of his patient's large four-post bed. Old Mr. Edward Mottisfont looked at him quizzically.

"How much would you take—eh, David? Come now—say—how much?"

David laughed again. His grey eyes twinkled. "Nary penny, sir," he said, swinging his arm over the great carved post beside him. There were cherubs' heads upon it, a fact that had always amused its owner considerably.

"Nonsense," said old Mr. Mottisfont, and for the first time his thin voice was tinged with earnestness. "Nonsense, David. Why! I've left you five thousand pounds."

David started. His eyes changed. They were very deep-set eyes. It was only when he laughed that they appeared grey. When he was serious they were so dark as to look black. Apparently he was moved and concerned. His voice took a boyish tone. "Oh, I say, sir—but you mustn't—I can't take it, you know."

"And why not, pray?" This was Mr. Mottisfont at his most sarcastic.

David got the better of his momentary embarrassment.

"I shan't forget that you've thought of it, sir," he said. "But I can't benefit under a patient's will. I haven't got many principles, but that's one of them. My father drummed it into me from the time I was about seven."

Old Mr. Edward Mottisfont lifted the thin eyebrows that had contrived to remain coal-black, although his hair was white. They gave him a Mephistophelean appearance of which he was rather proud.

"Very fine and highfalutin," he observed. "You 're an exceedingly upright young man, David."

David roared.

After a moment the old gentleman's lips gave way at the corners, and he laughed too.

"Oh, Lord, David, who'd ha' thought it of you!" he said. "You won't take a thousand?"

David shook his head.

"Not five hundred?"

David grinned.

"Not five pence," he said.

Old Mr. Mottisfont glared at him for a moment. "Prig," he observed with great conciseness. Then he pursed up his lips, felt under his pillow, and pulled out a long folded paper.

"All the more for Edward," he said maliciously. "All the more for Edward, and all the more reason for Edward to wish me dead. I wonder he don't poison me. Perhaps he will. Oh, Lord, I'd give something to see Edward tried for murder! Think of it, David—only think of it—Twelve British Citizens in one box—Edward in another—all the British Citizens looking at Edward, and Edward looking as if he was in church, and wondering if the moth was getting into his collections, and if any one would care for 'em when he was dead and gone. Eh, David? Eh, David? And Mary—like Niobe, all tears—"

David had been chuckling to himself, but at the mention of Edward's wife his face changed a little. He continued to laugh, but his eyes hardened, and he interrupted his patient: "Come, sir, you mustn't tire yourself."

"Like Niobe, all tears," repeated Mr. Mottisfont, obstinately. "Sweetly pretty she'd look too—eh, David? Edward's a lucky dog, ain't he?"

David's eyes flashed once and then hardened still more. His chin was very square.

"Come, sir," he repeated, and looked steadily at the old man.

"Beast—ain't I?" said old Mr. Mottisfont with the utmost cheerfulness. He occupied himself with arranging the bedclothes in an accurate line across his chest. As he did so, his hand touched the long folded paper, and he gave it an impatient push.

"You 're a damn nuisance, David," he said. "I've made my will once, and now I've to make it all over again just to please you. All the whole blessed thing over again, from 'I, Edward Morell Mottisfont,' down to 'I deliver this my act and deed.' Oh, Lord, what a bore."

"Mr. Fenwick," suggested David, and old Mr. Edward Mottisfont flared into sudden wrath.

"Don't talk to me of lawyers," he said violently. "I know enough law to make a will they can't upset. Don't talk of 'em. Sharks and robbers. Worse than the doctors. Besides young Fenwick talks—tells his wife things—and she tells her sister. And what Mary Bowden knows, the town knows. Did I ever tell you how I found out? I suspected, but I wanted to be sure. So I sent for young Fenwick, and told him I wanted to make my will. So far, so good. I made it—or he did. And I left a couple of thousand pounds to Bessie Fenwick and a couple more to her sister Mary in memory of my old friendship with their father. And as soon as Master Fenwick had gone I put his morning's work in the fire. Now how do I know he talked? This way. A week later I met Mary Bowden in the High

Street, and I had the fright of my life. I declare I thought she'd ha' kissed me. It was 'I hope you are prudent to be out in this east wind, dear Mr. Mottisfont,' and I must come and see them soon—and oh, Lord, what fools women are! Mary Bowden never could abide me till she thought I'd left her two thousand pounds."

"Fenwicks aren't the only lawyers in the world," suggested David.

"Much obliged, I'm sure. I did go to one once to make a will—they say it's sweet to play the fool sometimes—eh, David? Fool I was sure enough. I found a little mottled man, that sat blinking at me, and repeating my words, till I could have murdered him with his own office pen-knife. He called me Moral too, in stead of Morell. 'Edward Moral Mottisfont,' and I took occasion to inform him that I wasn't moral, never had been moral, and never intended to be moral. I said he must be thinking of my nephew Edward, who was damn moral. Oh, Lord, here is Edward. I could ha' done without him."

The door opened as he was speaking, and young Edward Mottisfont came in. He was a slight, fair man with a well-shaped head, a straight nose, and as much chin as a great many other people. He wore pince-nez because he was short-sighted, and high collars because he had a long neck. Both the pince-nez and the collar had an intensely irritating effect upon old Mr. Edward Mottisfont.

"If he hadn't been for ever blinking at some bug that was just out of his sight, his eyes would have been as good as mine, and he might just as well keep his head in a butterfly net or a collecting box as where he does keep it. Not that I should have said that Edward did keep his head."

"I think you flurry him, sir," said David, "and—"

"I know I do," grinned Mr. Mottisfont.

Young Edward Mottisfont came into the room and shut the door.

Old Mr. Mottisfont watched him with black, malicious eyes.

For as many years as Edward could remember anything, he could remember just that look upon his uncle's face. It made him uneasy now, as it had made him uneasy when he was only five years old.

Once when he was fifteen he said to David Blake: "You cheek him, David, and he likes you for it. How on earth do you manage it? Doesn't he make you feel beastly?"

And David stared and said: "Beastly? Rats! Why should I feel beastly? He's jolly amusing. He makes me laugh."

At thirty, Edward no longer employed quite the same ingenuous slang, but there was no doubt that he still experienced the same sensations, which fifteen years earlier he had characterized as beastly.

Old Mr. Edward Mottisfont lay in bed with his hands folded on his chest. He watched his nephew with considerable amusement, and waited for him to speak.

Edward took a chair beside the bed. Then he said that it was a fine day, and old Mr. Mottisfont nodded twice with much solemnity.

"Yes, Edward," he said.

There was a pause.

"I hope you are feeling pretty well," was the unfortunate Edward's next attempt at conversation.

Old Mr. Edward Mottisfont looked across at David Blake. "Am I feeling pretty well—eh, David?"

David laughed. He had moved when Edward came into the room, and was standing by the window looking out. A little square pane was open. Through it came the drowsy murmur of a drowsy, old-fashioned town. Mr. Mottisfont's house stood a few yards back from the road, just at the head of the High Street. Market Harford was a very old town, and the house was a very old house. There was a staircase which was admired by American visitors, and a front door for which they occasionally made bids. From where Mr. Mottisfont lay in bed he could see a narrow lane hedged in by high old houses with red tiles. Beyond, the ground fell sharply away, and there was a prospect of many red roofs. Farther still, beyond the river, he could see the great black chimneys of his foundry, and the smoke that came from them. It was the sight that he loved best in the world. David looked down into the High Street and watched one lamp after another spring into brightness. He could see a long ribbon of light go down to the river and then rise again. He turned back into the room when he was appealed to, and said:

"Why, you know best how you feel, sir."

"Oh, no," said old Mr. Mottisfont in a smooth, resigned voice. "Oh, no, David. In a private and unofficial sort of way, yes; but in a public and official sense, oh, dear, no. Edward wants to know when to order his mourning, and how to arrange his holiday so as not to clash with my funeral, so it is for my medical adviser to reply, ain't it, Edward?"

The colour ran to the roots of Edward Mottisfont's fair hair. He cast an appealing glance in David's direction, and did not speak.

"I don't think any of us will order our mourning till you 're dead, sir," said David with a chuckle. He commiserated Edward, but, after all, Edward was a lucky dog—and to see one's successful rival at a disadvantage is not an altogether unpleasant experience. "You'll outlive some of us young ones yet," he added, but old Mr. Mottisfont was frowning.

"Seen any more of young Stevenson, Edward?" he said, with an abrupt change of manner.

Edward shook his head rather ruefully.

"No, sir, I haven't."

"No, and you ain't likely to," said old Mr. Mottisfont. "There, you'd best be gone. I've talked enough."

"Then good-night, sir," said Edward Mottisfont, getting up with some show of cheerfulness.

The tone of Mr. Mottisfont's good-night was not nearly such a pleasant one, and as soon as the door had closed upon Edward he flung round towards David Blake with an angry "What's the good of him? What's the good of the fellow? He's not a business man. He's not a man at all; he's an entomologiac—a lepidoptofool—a damn lepidoptofool."

These remarkable epithets followed one another with an extraordinary rapidity.

When the old gentleman paused for breath David inquired, "What's the trouble, sir?"

"Oh, he's muddled the new contract with Stevenson. Thinking of butterflies, I expect. Pretty things, butterflies—but there—I don't see that I need distress myself. It ain't me it's going to touch. It's Edward's own look-out. My income ain't going to concern me for very much longer."

He was silent for a moment. Then he made a restless movement with his hand.

"It won't, will it—eh, David? You didn't mean what you said just now? It was just a flam? I ain't going to live, am I?"

David hesitated and the old man broke in with an extraordinary energy.

"Oh, for the Lord's sake, David, I 'm not a girl—out with it! How long d' ye give me?"

David sat down on the bed again. His movements had a surprising gentleness for so large a man. His odd, humorous face was quite serious.

"Really, sir, I don't know," he said, "I really don't. There's no more to be done if you won't let me operate. No, we won't go over all that again. I know you've made up your mind. And no one can possibly say how long it may be. You might have died this week, or you may die in a month, or it may go on for a year—or two—or three. You've the sort of constitution they don't make nowadays."

"Three years," said old Mr. Edward Mottisfont—"three years, David—and this damn pain all along—all the time—getting worse—"

"Oh, I think we can relieve the pain, sir," said David cheerfully.

"Much obliged, David. Some beastly drug that'll turn me into an idiot. No, thank ye, I'll keep my wits if it's all the same to you. Well, well, it's all in the day's work, and I 'm not complaining, but Edward'll get mortal tired of waiting for my shoes if I last three years. I doubt his patience holding out. He'll be bound to hasten matters on. Think of the bad example I shall be for the baby—when it comes. Lord, David, what d' ye want to look like that for? I suppose they'll have babies like other folk, and I'll be a bad example for 'em. Edward'll think of that. When he's thought of it enough, and I've got on his nerves a bit more than usual, he'll put strychnine or arsenic into my soup. Oh, Edward'll poison me yet. You'll see.'

"Poor old Edward, it's not much in his line," said David with half a laugh.

"Eh? What about Pellico's dog then?"

"Pellico's dog, sir?"

"What an innocent young man you are, David—never heard of Pellico's dog before, did you? Pellico's dog that got on Edward's nerves same as I get on his nerves, and you never knew that Edward dosed the poor brute with some of his bug-curing stuff, eh? To be sure you didn't think I knew, nor did Edward. I don't tell everything I know, and how I know it is my affair and none of yours, Master David Blake, but you see Edward's not so unhandy with a little job in the poisoning line."

David's face darkened. The incident of Pellico's dog had occurred when he and Edward were schoolboys of fifteen. He remembered it very well, but he did not very much care being reminded of it. Every day of his life he passed the narrow turning, down which, in defiance of parental prohibitions, he and Edward used to race each other to school. Old Pellico's dirty, evil-smelling shop still jutted out of the farther end, and the grimy door-step upon which his dog used to lie in wait for their ankles was still as grimy as ever. Sometimes it was a trouser-leg that suffered. Sometimes an ankle was nipped, and if Pellico's dog occasionally got a kick in return, it was not more than his due. David remembered his own surprise when it first dawned upon him that Edward minded—yes, actually minded these encounters. He recalled the occasion when Edward, his face of a suspicious pallor, had denied angrily that he was afraid of any beastly dog, and then his sudden wincing confession that he did mind—that he minded horribly—not because he was afraid of being bitten—Edward explained this point very carefully—but because the dog made such a beastly row, and because Edward dreamed of him at night, only in his dreams, Pellico's dog was rather larger than Pellico himself, and the lane was a cul-de-sac with a wall at the end of it, against which he crouched in his dream whilst the dog came nearer and nearer.

"What rot," was David's comment, "but if I felt like that, I jolly well know I'd knock the brute on the head."

"Would you?" said Edward, and that was all that had passed. Only, when a week later Pellico's dog was poisoned, David was filled with righteous indignation. He stormed at Edward.

"You did it—you know you did it. You did it with some of that beastly bug-killing stuff that you keep knocking about."

Edward was pale, but there was an odd gleam of triumph in the eyes that met David's.

"Well, you said you'd do for him—you said it yourself. So then I just did it."

David stared at him with all a schoolboy's crude condemnation of something that was "not the game."

"I'd have knocked him on the head under old Pellico's nose—but poison—poison's beastly."

He did not reason about it. It was just instinct. You knocked on the head a brute that annoyed you, but you didn't use poison. And Edward had used poison. That was the beginning of David's great intimacy with Elizabeth Chantrey. He did not quarrel with Edward, but they drifted out of an inseparable friendship into a relationship of the cool, go-as-you-please order. The thing rankled a little after all these years. David sat there frowning and remembering. Old Mr. Mottisfont laughed.

"Aha, you see I know most things," he said, "Edward'll poison me yet. You see, he's in a fix. He hankers after this house same as I always hankered after it. It's about the only taste we have in common. He's got his own house on a seven years' lease, and here's Nick Anderson going to be married, and willing to take it off his hands. And what's Edward to do? It's a terrible anxiety for him not knowing if I 'm going to die or not. If he doesn't accept Nick's offer and I die, he'll have two houses on his hands. If he accepts it and I don't die, he'll not have a house at all. It's a sad dilemma for Edward. That's why he would enjoy seeing about my funeral so much. He'd do it all very handsomely. Edward likes things handsome. And Mary, who doesn't care a jot for me, will wear a black dress that don't suit her, and feel like a Christian martyr. And Elizabeth won't wear black at all, though she cares a good many jots, and though she'd look a deal better in it than Mary—eh, David?"

But David Blake was exclaiming at the lateness of the hour, and saying good-night, all in a breath.

CHAPTER II

DAVID BLAKE

Grey, grey mist
  Over the old grey town,
A mist of years, a mist of tears,
  Where ghosts go up and down;
And the ghosts they whisper thus, and thus,
Of the days when the world went with us.

A MINUTE or two later Elizabeth Chantrey came into the room. She was a very tall woman, with a beautiful figure. All her movements were strong, sure, and graceful. She carried a lighted lamp in her left hand. Mr. Mottisfont abominated electric light and refused obstinately to have it in the house. When Elizabeth had closed the door and set down the lamp, she crossed over to the window and fastened a heavy oak shutter across it. Then she sat down by the bed.

"Well," she said in her pleasant voice.

"H'm," said old Mr. Mottisfont, "well or ill's all a matter of opinion, same as religion, or the cut of a dress." He shut his mouth with a snap, and lay staring at the ceiling. Presently his eyes wandered back to Elizabeth. She was sitting quite still, with her hands folded. Very few busy women ever sit still at all, but Elizabeth Chantrey, who was a very busy woman, was also a woman of a most reposeful presence. She could be unoccupied without appearing idle, just as she could be silent without appearing either stupid or constrained. Old Edward Mottisfont looked at her for about five minutes. Then he said suddenly:

"What'll you do when I 'm dead, Elizabeth?"

Elizabeth made no protest, as her sister Mary would have done. She had not been Edward Mottisfont's ward since she was fourteen for nothing. She understood him very well, and she was perhaps the one creature whom he really loved. She leaned her chin in her hand and said:

"I don't know, Mr. Mottisfont."

Mr. Mottisfont never took his eyes off her face.

"Edward'll want to move in here as soon as possible. What'll you do?"

"I don't know," repeated Elizabeth, frowning a little.

"Well, if you don't know, perhaps you'll listen to reason, and do as I ask you."

"If I can," said Elizabeth Chantrey.

He nodded.

"Stay here a year," he said, "a year isn't much to ask—eh?"

"Here?"

"Yes—in this house. I've spoken about it to Edward. Odd creature, Edward, but, I believe, truthful. Said he was quite agreeable. Even went so far as to say he was fond of you, and that Mary would be pleased. Said you'd too much tact to obtrude yourself, and that of course you'd keep your own rooms. No, I don't suppose you'll find it particularly pleasant, but I believe you'll find it worth while. Give it a year."

Elizabeth started ever so slightly. One may endure for years, and make no sign, to wince at last in one unguarded moment. So he knew—had always known. Again Elizabeth made no protest.

"A year," she said in a low voice, "a year—I've given fifteen years. Isn't fifteen years enough?"

Something fierce came into old Edward Mottisfont's eyes. His whole face hardened. "He's a damn fool," he said.

Elizabeth laughed.

"Of course he must be," and she laughed again.

The old man nodded.

"Grit," he said to himself, "grit. That's the way—laugh, Elizabeth, laugh—and let him go hang for a damn fool. He ain't worth it—no man living's worth it. But give him a year all the same."

If old Mr. Mottisfont had not been irritated with David Blake for being as he put it, a damn fool, he would not have made the references he had done to his nephew Edward's wife. They touched David upon the raw, and old Mr. Mottisfont was very well aware of it. As David went out of the room and closed the door, a strange mood came upon him. All the many memories of this house, familiar to him from early boyhood, all the many memories of this town of his birth and upbringing, rose about him. It was a strange mood, but yet not a sad one, though just beyond it lay the black shadow which is the curse of the Celt. David Blake came of an old Irish stock, although he had never seen Ireland. He had the vein of poetry—the vein of sadness, which are born at a birth with Irish humour and Irish wit.

As he went down the staircase, the famous staircase with its carved newels, the light of a moving lamp came up from below, and at the turn of the stair he stood aside to let Elizabeth Chantrey pass. She wore a grey dress, and the lamp-light shone upon her hair and made it look like very pale gold. It was thick hair—very fine and thick, and she wore it in a great plait like a crown. In the daytime it was not golden at all, but just the colour of the pale thick honey with which wax is mingled. Long ago a Chantrey had married a wife from Norway with Elizabeth's hair and Elizabeth's dark grey eyes.

"Good-night, David," said Elizabeth Chantrey. She would have passed on, but to her surprise David made no movement. He was looking at her.

"This is where I first saw you, Elizabeth," he said in a remembering voice. "You had on a grey dress, like that one, but Mary was in blue, because Mr. Mottisfont wouldn't let her wear mourning. Do you remember how shocked poor Miss Agatha was?—'and their mother only dead a month!' I can hear her now." Mary—yes, he remembered little Mary Chantrey in her blue dress. He could see her now—nine years old—in a blue dress—with dark curling hair and round brown eyes, holding tightly to Elizabeth's skirts, and much too shy to speak to the big strange boy who was Edward's friend.

Elizabeth watched him. She knew very well that he was not thinking of her, although he had remembered the grey dress. And yet—for five years—it was she and not Mary to whom David came with every mood. During those five years, the years between fourteen and nineteen, it was always Elizabeth and David, David and Elizabeth. Then when David was twenty, and in his first year at hospital, Dr. Blake died suddenly, and for four years David came no more to Market Harford. Mrs. Blake went to live with a sister in the north, and David's vacations were spent with his mother. For a time he wrote often—then less often—finally only at Christmas. And the years passed, Elizabeth's girlhood passed, Mary grew up. And when David Blake had been nearly three years qualified, and young

Dr. Ellerton was drowned out boating, David bought from Mrs. Ellerton a share in the practice that had been his father's, and brought his mother back to Market Harford. Mrs. Blake lived only for a year, but before she died she had seen David fall headlong in love, not with her dear Elizabeth, but with Mary—pretty little Mary—who was turning the heads of all the young men, sending Jimmy Larkin with a temporarily broken heart to India, Jack Webster with a much more seriously injured one to the West Coast of Africa, and enjoying herself mightily the while. Elizabeth had memories as well as David. They came at least as near sadness as his. She thought she had remembered quite enough for one evening, and she set her foot on the stair above the landing.

"Poor Miss Agatha!" she said. "What a worry we were to her, and how she disliked our coming here. I can remember her grumbling to Mr. Mottisfont, and saying, 'Children make such a work in the house,' and Mr. Mottisfont—"

Elizabeth laughed.

"Mr. Mottisfont said, 'Don't be such a damn old maid, Agatha. For the Lord's sake, what's the good of a woman that can't mind children?'"

David laughed too. He remembered Miss Agatha's fussy indignation.

"Good-night, David," said Elizabeth, and she passed on up the wide, shallow stair.

The light went with her. From below there came only a glimmer, for the lamp in the hall was still turned low. David went slowly on. As he was about to open the front door, Edward Mottisfont came out of the dining-room on the left.

"One minute, David," he said, and took him by the arm. "Look here—I think I ought to know. Is my uncle likely to live on indefinitely? Did you mean what you said upstairs?"

It was the second time that David Blake had been asked if he meant those words. He answered a trifle irritably.

"Why should I say what I don't mean? He may live three years or he may die to-morrow. Why on earth should I say it if I didn't think it?"

"Oh, I don't know," said Edward. "You might have been saying it just to cheer the old man up."

There was a certain serious simplicity about Edward Mottisfont. It was this quality in him which his uncle stigmatized as priggishness. Your true prig is always self-conscious, but Edward was not at all self-conscious. From his own point of view he saw things quite clearly. It was other people's points of view which had a confusing effect upon him. David laughed.

"It didn't exactly cheer him up," he said. "He isn't as set on living as all that comes to."

Edward appeared to be rather struck by this statement.

"Isn't he?" he said.

He opened the door as he spoke, but suddenly closed it again. His tone altered. It became eager and boyish.

"David, I say—you know Jimmy Larkin was transferred to Assam some months ago? Well, I wrote and asked him to remember me if he came across anything like specimens. Of course his forest work gives him simply priceless opportunities. He wrote back and said he would see what he could do, and last mail he sent me—"

"What—a package of live scorpions?"

"No—not specimens—oh, if he could only have sent the specimen—but it was the next best thing—a drawing—you remember how awfully well Jimmy drew—a coloured drawing of a perfectly new slug."

Edward's tone became absolutely ecstatic. He began to rumple up his fair hair, as he always did when he was excited. "I can't find it in any of the books," he said, "and they'd never even heard of it at the Natural History Museum. Five yellow bands on a black ground—what do you think of that?

"I should say it was Jimmy, larking," murmured David, getting the door open and departing hastily, but Edward was a great deal too busy wondering whether the slug ought in justice to be called after Jimmy, or whether he might name it after himself, to notice this ribaldry.

David Blake came out into a clear September night. The sky was cloudless and the air was still. Presently there would be a moon. David walked down the brightly-lighted High Street, with its familiar shops. Here and there were a few new names, but for the most part he had known them all from childhood. Half-way down the hill he passed the tall grey house which had once had his father's plate upon the door—the house where David was born. Old Mr. Bull lived there now, his father's partner once, retired these eighteen months in favour of his nephew, Tom Skeffington. All Market Harford wondered what Dr. Bull could possibly want with a house so much too large for him. He used only half the rooms, and the house had a sadly neglected air, but there were days, and this was one of them, when David, passing, could have sworn that the house had not changed hands at all and that the blind of his mother's room was lifted a little as he went by. She used to wave to him from that window as he came from school. She wore the diamond ring which David kept locked up in his dispatch-box. Sometimes it caught the light and flashed. David could have sworn that he saw it flash to-night. But the house was all dark and silent. The old days were gone. David walked on.

At the bottom of the High Street, just before you come to the bridge, he turned up to the right, where a paved path with four stone posts across the entrance came into the High Street at right angles. The path ran along above the river, with a low stone wall to the left, and a row of grey stone houses to the right. Between the wall and the river there were trees, which made a pleasant shade in the summer. Now they were losing their leaves. David opened the door of the seventh house with his latch-key, and went in. That night he dreamed his dream. It was a long time now since he had dreamed it, but it was an old dream—one that recurred from time to time—one that had come to him at intervals for as long as he could remember. And it was always the same—through all the years it never varied—it was always just the same.

He dreamed that he was standing upon the seashore. It was a wide, low shore, with a long, long stretch of sand that shone like silver under a silver moon. It shone because it was wet, still quite wet from the touch of the tide. The tide was very low. David stood on the shore, and saw the moon go down into the sea. As it went down it changed slowly. It became golden, and the sand turned golden too. A wind began to blow in from the sea. A wind from the west—a wind that was strong, and yet very gentle. At the edge of the sea there stood a woman, with long, floating hair and a long floating dress. She stood between David and the golden moon, and the wind blew out her dress and her long floating hair. But David never saw her face. Always he longed to see her face, but he never saw it. He stood upon the shore and could not move to go to her. When he was a boy he used to walk in his sleep in the nights when he had this dream. Once he was awakened by the touch of cold stones under his bare feet. And there he stood, just as he had come from bed, on the wet door-step, with the front door open behind him. After that he locked his door. Now he walked in his sleep no longer, and it was more than a year since he had dreamed the dream at all, but to-night it came to him again.

CHAPTER III

DEAD MEN'S SHOES

There's many a weary game to be played
With never a penny to choose,
But the weariest game in all the world
Is waiting for dead men's shoes.

IT was about a week later that Edward Mottisfont rang David Blake up on the telephone and begged him in agitated accents, to come to Mr. Mottisfont without delay.

"It's another attack—a very bad one," said Edward in the hall. His voice shook a little, and he seemed very nervous. David thought it was certainly a bad attack. He also thought it a strange one. The old man was in great pain, and very ill. Elizabeth Chantrey was in the room, but after a glance at his patient, David sent her away. As she went she made a movement to take up an empty cup which stood on the small table beside the bed, and old Mr. Edward Mottisfont fairly snapped at her.

"Leave it, will you—I've stopped Edward taking it twice. Leave it, I say!"

Elizabeth went out without a word, and Mr. Mottisfont caught David's wrist in a shaky grip.

"D' you know why I wouldn't let her take that cup? D' you know why?"

"No, sir—"

Old Mr. Mottisfont's voice dropped to a thread. He was panting a little.

"I was all right till I drank that damned tea, David," he said, "and Edward brought it to me—Edward—"

"Come, sir—come—" said David gently. He was really fond of this queer old man, and he was distressed for him.

"David, you won't let him give me things—you'll look to it. Look in the cup. I wouldn't let 'em take the cup—there's dregs. Look at 'em, David."

David took up the cup and walked to the window. About a tablespoonful of cold tea remained. David tilted the cup, then became suddenly attentive. That small remainder of cold tea with the little skim of cream upon it had suddenly become of absorbing interest. David tilted the cup still more. The tea made a little pool on one side of it, and all across the bottom of the cup a thick white sediment drained slowly down into the pool. It was such a sediment as is left by very chalky water. But all the water of Market Harford is as soft as rain-water. It is not only chalk that makes a sediment like that. Arsenic makes one, too. David put down the cup quickly. He opened the door and went out into the passage. From the far end Elizabeth Chantrey came to meet him, and he gave her a hastily scribbled note for the chemist, and asked her for one or two things that were in the house. When he came back into Mr. Mottisfont's room he went straight to the wash-stand, took up a small glass bottle labeled ipecacuanha wine and spent two or three minutes in washing it thoroughly. Then he poured into it very carefully the contents of the cup. He did all this in total silence, and in a very quiet and business-like manner.

Old Mr. Edward Mottisfont lay on his right side and watched him. His face was twisted with pain, and there was a dampness upon his brow, but his eyes followed every motion that David made and noted every look upon his face. They were intent—alive—observant. Whilst David stood by the wash-stand, with his back towards the bed, old Mr.

Edward Mottisfont's lips twisted themselves into an odd smile. A gleam of sardonic humour danced for a moment in the watching eyes. When David put down the bottle and came over to the bed, the gleam was gone, and there was only pain—great pain—in the old, restless face. There was a knock at the door, and Elizabeth Chantrey came in.

Three hours later David Blake came out of the room that faced old Mr. Mottisfont's at the farther end of the corridor. It was a long, low room, fitted up as a laboratory—very well and fully fitted up—for the old man had for years found his greatest pleasure and relaxation in experimenting with chemicals. Some of his experiments he confided to David, but the majority he kept carefully to himself. They were of a somewhat curious nature. David Blake came out of the laboratory with a very stern look upon his face. As he went down the stair he met with Edward Mottisfont coming up. The sternness intensified. Edward looked an unspoken question, and then without a word turned and went down before David into the hall. Then he waited.

"Gone?" he said in a sort of whisper, and David bent his head.

He was remembering that it was only a week since he had told Edward in this very spot that his uncle might live for three years. Well, he was dead now. The old man was dead now—out of the way—some one had seen to that. Who? David could still hear Edward Mottisfont's voice asking, "How long is he likely to live?" and his own answer, "Perhaps three years."

"Come in here," said Edward Mottisfont. He opened the dining-room door as he spoke, and David followed him into a dark, old-fashioned room, separated from the one behind it by folding-doors. One of the doors stood open about an inch, but there was only one lamp in the room, and neither of the two men paid any attention to such a trifling circumstance.

Edward sat down by the table, which was laid for dinner. Even above the white tablecloth his face was noticeably white. All his life this old man had been his bugbear. He had hated him, not with the hot hatred which springs from one great sudden wrong, but with the cold slow abhorrence bred of a thousand trifling oppressions. He had looked forward to his death. For years he had thought to himself, "Well, he can't live for ever." But now that the old man was dead, and the yoke lifted from his neck, he felt no relief—no sense of freedom. He felt oddly shocked.

David Blake did not sit down. He stood at the opposite side of the table and looked at Edward. From where he stood he could see first the white tablecloth, then Edward's face, and on the wall behind Edward, a full-length portrait of old Edward Mottisfont at the age of thirty. It was the work of a young man whom Market Harford had looked upon as a very disreputable young man. He had since become so famous that they had affixed a tablet to the front of the house in which he had once lived. The portrait was one of the best he had ever painted, and the eyes, Edward Mottisfont's black, malicious eyes, looked down from the wall at his nephew, and at David Blake. Neither of the men had spoken since they entered the room, but they were both so busy with their thoughts that neither noticed how silent the other was.

At last David spoke. He said in a hard level voice:

"Edward, I can't sign the certificate. There will have to be an inquest."

Edward Mottisfont looked up with a great start.

"An inquest?" he said, "an inquest?"

One of David's hands rested on the table. "I can't sign the certificate," he repeated.

Edward stared at him.

"Why not?" he said. "I don't understand—"

"Don't you?" said David Blake.

Edward rumpled up his hair in a distracted fashion.

"I don't understand," he repeated. "An inquest? Why, you've been attending him all these months, and you said he might die at any time. You said it only the other day. I don't understand—"

"Nor do I," said David curtly.

Edward stared again.

"What do you mean?"

"Mr. Mottisfont might have lived for some time," said David Blake, speaking slowly. "I was attending him for a chronic illness, which would have killed him sooner or later. But it didn't kill him. It didn't have a chance. He died of poisoning—arsenic poisoning."

One of Edward's hands was lying on the table. His whole arm twitched, and the hand fell over, palm upwards. The fingers opened and closed slowly. David found himself staring at that slowly moving hand.

"Impossible," said Edward, and his breath caught in his throat as he said it.

"I 'm afraid not."

Edward leaned forward a little.

"But, David," he said, "it's not possible. Who—who do you think—who would do such a thing. Or—suicide—do you think he committed suicide?"

David drew himself suddenly away from the table. All at once the feeling had come to him that he could no longer touch what Edward touched.

"No, I don't think it was suicide," he said. "But of course it's not my business to think at all. I shall give my evidence, and there, as far as I am concerned, the matter ends."

Edward looked helplessly at David.

"Evidence?" he repeated.

"At the inquest," said David Blake.

"I don't understand," said Edward again. He put his head in his hands, and seemed to be thinking.

"Are you sure?" he said at last. "I don't see how—it was an attack—just like his other attacks—and then he died—you always said he might die in one of those attacks."

There was a sort of trembling eagerness in Edward's tone. A feeling of nausea swept over David. The scene had become intolerable.

"Mr. Mottisfont died because he drank a cup of tea which contained enough arsenic to kill a man in robust health," he said sharply.

He looked once at Edward, saw him start, and added, "and I think that you brought him that tea."

"Yes," said Edward. "He asked me for it, how could there be arsenic in it?"

"There was," said David Blake.

"Arsenic? But I brought him the tea—"

"Yes, you brought him the tea."

Edward lifted his head. His eyes behind his glasses had a misty and bewildered look. His voice shook a little.

"But—if there's an inquest—they might say—they might think—"

He pushed his chair back a little way, and half rose from it, resting his hands on the table, and peering across it.

"David, why do you look at me like that?"

David Blake turned away.

"It's none of my business," he said, "I've got to give my evidence, and for God's sake, Edward, pull yourself together before the inquest, and get decent legal advice, for you'll need it."

Edward was shockingly pale.

"You mean—what do you mean? That people will think—it's impossible."

David went towards the door. His face was like a flint.

"I mean this," he said. "Mr. Mottisfont died of arsenic poisoning. The arsenic was in a cup of tea which he drank. You brought him the tea. You are undoubtedly in a very serious position. There will have to be an inquest."

Edward had risen completely. He made a step towards David.

"But if you were to sign the certificate—there wouldn't need to be an inquest—David—"

"But I 'm damned if I'll sign the certificate," said David Blake.

He went out and shut the door sharply behind him.

CHAPTER IV

A MAN'S HONOUR

"Will you give me your heart?" she said.
"Oh, I gave it you long ago," said he.
"Why, then, I threw it away," said she.
"And what will you give me instead?
Will you give me your honour?" she said.

"ELIZABETH!"

There was a pause.

"Elizabeth—open your door!"

Elizabeth Chantrey came back from a long way off. Mary was calling her. Mary was knocking at her door. She got up rather wearily, turned the key, and with a little gasp, Mary was in the room, shutting the door, and standing with her back against it. The lamp burned low, but Elizabeth's eyes were accustomed to the gloom. Mary Mottisfont's bright, clear colour was one of her great attractions. It was all gone and her dark eyes looked darker and larger than they should have done.

"Why, Molly, I thought you had gone home. Edward told me he was sending you home an hour ago."

"He told me to go," said Mary in a sort of stumbling whisper. "He told me to go—but I wanted to wait and go with him. I knew he'd be upset—I knew he'd feel it—when it was all over. I wanted to be with him—oh, Liz—"

"Mary, what is it?"

Mary put up a shaking hand.

"I'll tell you—don't stop me—there's no time—I'll tell you—oh, I 'm telling you as fast as I can."

She spoke in a series of gasps.

"I went into your little room behind the dining-room. I knew no one would come. I knew I should hear any one coming or going. I opened the door into the dining-room— just a little—"

"Mary, what is it?" said Elizabeth. She put her arm round her sister, but Mary pushed her away.

"Don't—there's no time. Let me go on. David came down. He came into the dining-room. He talked to Edward. He said, 'I can't sign the certificate,' and Edward said, 'Why not?' and David said, 'Because'—Liz—I can't—oh, Liz, I can't—I can't."

Mary caught suddenly at Elizabeth's arm and began to sob. She had no tears—only hard sobs. Her pretty oval face was all white and drawn. There were dark marks like bruises under her hazel eyes. The little dark rings of hair about her forehead were damp.

"Dearest—darling—my Molly dear," said Elizabeth. She held Mary to her, with strong supporting arms, but the shuddering sobs went on.

"Liz—it was poison. He says it was poison. He says there was poison in the tea— arsenic poison—and Edward took him the tea. Liz—Liz, why do such awful things happen? Why does God let them happen?"

Elizabeth was much taller than her sister—taller and stronger. She released herself from the clutching fingers, and let both her hands fall suddenly and heavily upon Mary's shoulders.

"Molly, what are you talking about?" she cried.

Mary was startled into a momentary self-control.

"Mr. Mottisfont," she said. "David said it was poison—poison, Liz."

Her voice fell to a low horrified whisper at the word, and then rose on the old gasp of, "Edward took him the tea." A numbness came upon Elizabeth. Feeling was paralysed. She was conscious neither of horror, anxiety, nor sorrow. Only her brain remained clear. All her consciousness seemed to have gone to it, and it worked with an inconceivable clearness and rapidity.

"Hush, Mary," she said. "What are you saying? Edward—"

Mary pushed her away.

"Of course not," she said. "Liz, if you dared—but you don't—no one could really—Edward of all people. But there's all the talk, the scandal—we can't have it. It must be stopped. And we 're losing time, we 're losing time dreadfully. I must go to David, and stop him before he writes to any one, or sees any one. He must sign the certificate."

Elizabeth stood quite still for a moment. Then she went to the wash-stand, poured out a glass of water, and came back to Mary.

"Drink this, Molly," she said. "Yes, drink it all, and pull yourself together. Now listen to me. You can't possibly go to David."

"I must go, I must," said Mary. Her tone hardened. "Will you come with me, Liz, or must I go alone?"

Elizabeth took the empty glass and set it down.

"Molly, my dear, you must listen. No—I 'm thinking of what's best for every one. You don't want any talk. If you go to David's house at this hour—well, you can see for yourself. No—listen, my dear. If I ring David up, and ask him to come here at once—at once—to see me, don't you see how much better that will be?"

Mary's colour came and went. She stood irresolute.

"Very well," she said at last. "If he'll come. If he won't, then I'll go to him, and I don't care what you say, Elizabeth—and you must be quick—quick."

They went downstairs in silence. Mr. Mottisfont's study was in darkness, and Elizabeth brought in the lamp from the hall, holding it very steadily. Then she sat down at the great littered desk and rang up the exchange. She gave the number and they waited. After what seemed like a very long time, Elizabeth heard David's voice.

"Hullo!"

"It is I—Elizabeth," said Elizabeth Chantrey.

"What is it?"

"Can you come here at once? I want to see you at once. Yes, it is very important—important and urgent."

Mary was in an agony of impatience. "What does he say? Will he come at once?"

But Elizabeth answered David and not her sister.

"No, presently won't do. It must be at once. It's really urgent, David, or I wouldn't ask it. Yes, thank you so much. In my room."

She put down the receiver, rang off, and turned to Mary.

"He is coming. Had you not better send Edward a message, or he will be coming back here? Ring up, and say that you are staying with me for an hour, and that Markham will walk home with you."

In Elizabeth's little brown room the silence weighed and the time lagged. Mary walked up and down, moving perpetually—restlessly—uselessly. There was a small Dutch mirror above the writing-table. Its cut glass border caught the light, and reflected it in diamond points and rainbow flashes. It was the brightest thing in the room. Mary stood for a moment and looked at her own face. She began to arrange her hair with nervous, trembling fingers. She rubbed her cheeks, and straightened the lace at her throat. Then she fell to pacing up and down again.

"The room's so hot," she said suddenly. And she went quickly to the window and flung it open. The air came in, cold and mournfully damp. Mary drew half a dozen long breaths. Then she shivered, her teeth chattered. She shut the window with a jerk, and as she did so David Blake came into the room. It was Elizabeth he saw, and it was to Elizabeth that he spoke.

"Is anything the matter? Anything fresh?" Elizabeth moved aside, and all at once he saw Mary Mottisfont.

"Mary wants to speak to you," said Elizabeth. She made a step towards the door, but Mary called her sharply. "No, Liz—stay!"

And Elizabeth drew back into the shadowed corner by the window, whilst Mary came forward into the light. For a moment there was silence. Mary's hands were clasped before her, her chin was a little lifted, her eyes were desperately intent.

"David," she said in a low fluttering voice, "Oh, David—I was in here—I heard—I could not help hearing."

"What did you hear?" asked David Blake. The words came from him with a sort of startled hardness.

"I heard everything you said to Edward—about Mr. Mottisfont. You said it was poison. I heard you say it."

"Yes," said David Blake.

"And Edward took him the tea," said Mary quickly. "Don't you see, David—don't you see how dreadful it is for Edward? People who didn't know him might say—they might think such dreadful things—and if there were an inquest—" the words came in a sort of strangled whisper. "There can't be an inquest—there can't. Oh, David, you'll sign the certificate, won't you?"

David's face had been changing while she spoke. The first hard startled look went from it. It was succeeded by a flash of something like horror, and then by pain—pain and a great pity.

"No, Mary, dear, I can't," he said very gently. He looked at her, and further words died upon his lips. Mary came nearer. There was a big chair in front of the fireplace, and she rested one hand on the back of it. It seemed as if she needed something firm to touch, her world was shifting so. David had remained standing by the door, but Mary was not a yard away from him now.

"You see, David," she said, still in that low tremulous voice, "you see, David, you haven't thought—you can't have thought—what it will mean if you don't. Edward might be suspected of a most dreadful thing. I 'm sure you haven't thought of that. He might even"—Mary's eyes widened—"he might even be *arrested*—and tried—and I couldn't *bear* it." The hand that rested on the chair began to tremble very much. "I couldn't bear it," said Mary piteously.

"Mary, my dear," said David, "this is a business matter, and you mustn't interfere—I can't possibly sign the certificate. Poor old Mr. Mottisfont did not die a natural death, and the matter will have to be inquired into. No innocent person need have anything to be afraid of."

"Oh!" said Mary. Her breath came hard. "You haven't told any one—not yet? You haven't written? Oh, am I too late? Have you told people already?"

"No." said David, "not yet, but I must."

The tears came with a rush to Mary's eyes, and began to roll down her cheeks.

"No, no, David, no," she said. Her left hand went out towards him gropingly. "Oh, no, David, you mustn't. You haven't thought—indeed you haven't. Innocent people can't always prove that they are innocent. They *can't*. There's a book—a dreadful book. I've just been reading it. There was a man who was quite, quite innocent—as innocent as Edward—and he couldn't prove it. And they were going to hang him—David!"

Mary's voice broke off with a sort of jerk. Her face became suddenly ghastly. There was an extremity of terror in every sharpened feature. Elizabeth stood quite straight and still by the window. She was all in shadow, her brown dress lost against the soft brown gloom of the half-drawn velvet curtain. She felt like a shadow herself as she looked and listened. The numbness was upon her still. She was conscious as it were of a black cloud that overshadowed them all—herself, Mary, Edward. But not David. David stood just beyond, and Mary was trying to hold him and to draw him into the blackness. Something in Elizabeth's deadened consciousness kept saying over and over again: "Not David, not David." Elizabeth saw the black cloud with a strange internal vision. With her bodily eyes she watched David's face. She saw it harden when Mary looked at him, and quiver with pain when she looked away. She saw his hand go out and touch Mary's hand, and she heard him say:

"Mary, I can't. Don't ask me."

Mary put her other hand suddenly on David's wrist. A bright colour flamed into her cheeks.

"David, you used to be fond of me—once—not long ago. You said you would do anything for me. Anything in the world. You said you loved me. And you said that nowadays a man did not get the opportunity of showing a woman what he would do for her. You wanted to do something for me then, and I had nothing to ask you. Aren't you fond of me any more, David? Won't you do anything for me now?—now that I ask you?"

David pulled his hand roughly from her grasp. He pushed past her, and crossed the room.

"Mary, you don't know what you are asking me," he said in a tone of sharp exasperation. "You don't know what you are talking about. You don't seem to realize that you are asking me to become an accessory after the fact in a case of murder."

Mary shuddered. The word was like a blow. She spoke in a hurried whispering way.

"But Edward—it's for Edward. What will happen to Edward? And to me? Don't you care? We've only been married six months. It's such a little time. Don't you care at all? I never knew such dreadful things could happen—not to one's self. You read things in papers, and you never think—you never, never think that a thing like that could happen to yourself. I suppose those people don't all die, but I should die. Oh, David, aren't you going to help us?"

She spoke the last words as a child might have spoken them. Her eyes were fixed appealingly upon David's face. Mary Mottisfont had very beautiful eyes. They were hazel in colour, and in shape and expression they resembled those of another Mary, who was also Queen of Hearts.

Elizabeth Chantrey became suddenly aware that she was shaking all over, and that the room was full of a thick white mist. She groped in the mist and found a chair. She made a step forward, and sat down. Then the mist grew thinner by degrees, and through it she saw that Mary had come quite close to David again. She was looking up at him. Her hands were against his breast, and she was saying:

"David—David—David, you said the world was not enough to give me once."

David's face was rigid.

"You wouldn't take what I had to give," he said very low. He had forgotten Elizabeth Chantrey. He saw nothing but Mary's eyes.

"You didn't want my love, Mary, and now you want my honour. And you say it is only a little thing."

Mary lifted her head and met his eyes.

"Give it me," she said. "If it is a great thing, well, I shall value it all the more. Oh, David, because I ask it. Because I shall love you all my life, and bless you all my life. And if I 'm asking you a great thing—oh, David, you said that nothing would be too great to give me. Oh, David, won't you give me this now? Won't you give me this one thing, because I ask it?"

As Mary spoke the mist cleared from before Elizabeth's eyes and the numbness that had been upon her changed slowly into feeling. She put both hands to her heart, and held them there. Her heart beat against her hands, and every beat hurt her. She felt again, and what she felt was the sharpest pain that she had ever known, and she had known much pain.

She had suffered when David left Market Harford. She had suffered when he ceased to write. She had suffered when he returned only to fall headlong in love with Mary. And what she had suffered then had been a personal pang, a thing to be struggled with, dominated, and overcome. Now she must look on whilst David suffered too. Must watch whilst his nerves tautened, his strength failed, his self-control gave way. And she could not shut her eyes or look away. She could not raise her thought above this level of pain. The black cloud overshadowed them and hid the light of heaven.

"Because I ask you, David—David, because I ask you."

Mary's voice trembled and fell to a quivering whisper.

Suddenly David pushed her away. He turned and made a stumbling step towards the fireplace. His hands gripped the narrow mantelshelf. His eyes stared at the wall. And from the wall Mary's eyes looked back at him from the miniature of Mary's mother. There was a long minute's silence. Then David swung round. His face was flushed, his eyes looked black.

"If I do it can you hold your tongues?" he said in a rough, harsh voice.

Mary drew a deep soft breath of relief. She had won. Her hands dropped to her side, her whole figure relaxed, her face became soft and young again.

"O David, God bless you!" she cried.

David frowned. His brows made a dark line across his face. Every feature was heavy and forbidding.

"Can you hold your tongues?" he repeated. "Do you understand—do you fully understand that if a word of this is ever to get out it's just sheer ruin to the lot of us? Do you grasp that?"

Elizabeth Chantrey got up. She crossed the room, and stood at David's side, nearly as tall as he.

"Don't do it, David," she said, with a sudden passion in her voice.

Mary turned on her in a flash.

"Liz," she cried; but David stood between.

"It's none of your business, Elizabeth. You keep out of it." The tone was kinder than the words.

Elizabeth was silent. She drew away, and did not speak again.

"I'll do it on one condition," said David Blake. "You'd better go and tell Edward at once. I don't want to see him. I don't suppose he's been talking to any one—it's not exactly likely—but if he has the matter's out of my hands. I'll not touch it. If he hasn't and you'll all hold your tongues, I'll do it."

He turned to the door and Mary cried: "Won't you write it now? Won't you sign it before you go?"

David laughed grimly.

"Do you think I go about with my pockets full of death certificates?" he said. Then he was gone, and the door shut to behind him.

Elizabeth moved, and spoke.

"I will tell Markham that you are ready to go home," she said.

CHAPTER V

TOWN TALK

As long as idle dogs will bark, and idle asses bray,
As long as hens will cackle over every egg they lay,
   So long will folks be chattering,
   And idle tongues be clattering,
For the less there is to talk about, the more there is to say.

THE obituary notices of old Mr. Mottisfont which appeared in due course in the two local papers were of a glowingly appreciative nature, and at least as accurate as such notices usually are. David could not help thinking how much the old gentleman would have relished the fine phrases and the flowing periods. Sixty years of hard work were compressed into two and a half columns of palpitating journalese. David preferred the old man's own version, which had fewer adjectives and a great deal more backbone.

"My father left me nothing but debts—and William. The ironworks were in a bad way, and we were on the edge of a bankruptcy. I was twenty-one, and William was fifteen, and every one shook their heads. I can see 'em now. Well, I gave some folk the rough side of my tongue, and some the smooth. I had to have money, and no one would lend. I got a little credit, but I couldn't get the cash. Then I hunted up my father's cousin, Edward Moberly. Rolling he was, and as close as wax. Bored to death too, for all his money. I talked to him, and he took to me. I talked to him for three days, and he lent me what I wanted, on my note of hand, and I paid it all back in five years, and the interest up-to-date right along. It took some doing but I got it done. Then the thing got a go on it, and we climbed right up. And folks stopped shaking their heads. I began to make my mark. I began to be a 'respected fellow-citizen.' Oh, Lord, David, if you'd known William you'd respect me too! Talk about the debts—as a handicap, they weren't worth mentioning in the same breath with William. I could talk people into believing I was solvent, but I couldn't talk 'em into believing that William had any business capacity. And I couldn't pay off William, same as I paid off the debts."

David's recollections plunged him suddenly into a gulf of black depression. Such a plucky old man, and now he was dead—out of the way—and he, David, had lent a hand to cover the matter over, and shield the murderer. David took the black fit to bed with him at night, and rose in the morning with the gloom upon him still. It became a shadow which went with him in all his ways and clung about his every thought. And with the gloom there came upon him a horrible, haunting recurrence of his old passion for Mary. The wound made by her rejection of him had been slowly skinning over, but in the scene which they had shared, and the stress of the emotions raised by it, this wound had broken out afresh, and now it was no more a deep clean cut, but a festering thing that bid fair to poison all the springs of life. At Mary's bidding he had violated a trust, and his own sense of honour. There were times when he hated Mary. There were times when he craved for her. And always his contempt for himself deepened, and with it the gloom—the black gloom.

"The doctor gets through a sight of whisky these days," remarked Mrs. Havergill, David's housekeeper. "And a more abstemious gentleman, I 'm sure I never did live with. Weeks a bottle of whisky 'ud last, unless he'd friends in. And now—gone like a flash, as you might say. Only, just you mind there's not a word of this goes out of the 'ouse, Sarah, my girl. D' ye hear?"

Sarah, a whey-faced girl whose arms and legs were set on at uncertain angles, only nodded. She adored David with the unreasoning affection of a dog, and had he taken to washing in whisky instead of merely drinking it, she would have regarded his doing so as quite a right and proper thing.

When the local papers had finished Mr. Mottisfont's obituary notices and had lavished all their remaining stock of adjectives upon the funeral arrangements, they proceeded to interest themselves in the terms of his will. For once, old Mr. Mottisfont had done very much what was expected of him. Local charities benefited and old servants were remembered. Elizabeth Chantrey was left twenty-five thousand pounds, and everything else went to Edward. "To David Blake I leave my sincere respect, he having declined to receive a legacy."

David could almost see the old man grin as he wrote the words, could almost hear him chuckle, "Very well, my highfalutin young man—into the pillory with you."

The situation held a touch of sardonic humour beyond old Mr. Mottisfont's contriving, and the iron of it rusted into David's soul. Market Harford discussed the terms of the will with great interest. They began to speculate as to what Elizabeth Chantrey would do. When it transpired that she was going to remain on in the old house and be joined there by Edward and Mary, there was quite a little buzz of talk.

"I assure you he make it a condition—a secret condition," said old Mrs. Codrington in her deep booming voice. "I have it from Mary herself. He made it a condition."

It was quite impossible to disbelieve a statement made with so much authority. Mrs. Codrington's voice always stood her in good stead. It had a solidity which served to prop up any shaky fact. Miss Dobell, to whom she was speaking, sniffed, and felt a little out of it. She had been Agatha Mottisfont's great friend, and as such she felt that she herself should have been the fountainhead of information. As soon as Mrs. Codrington had departed Miss Hester Dobell put on her outdoor things and went to call upon Mary Mossitfont.

As it was a damp afternoon, she pinned up her skirts all round, and she was still unpinning them upon Mary's doorstep, when the door opened.

"Miss Chantrey is with her sister? Oh, indeed! That is very nice, very nice indeed. And Mrs. Mottisfont is seeing visitors, you say? Yes? Then I will just walk in—just walk in."

Miss Dobell came into the drawing-room with a little fluttered run. Her faded blue eyes were moist, but not so moist as to prevent her perceiving that Mary wore a black dress which did not become her, and that Elizabeth had on an old grey coat and skirt, with dark furs, and a close felt hat which almost hid her hair. She greeted Mary very affectionately and Elizabeth a shade less affectionately.

"I hope you are well, Mary, my dear? Yes? That is good. These sad times are very trying. And you, Elizabeth? I am pleased to find that you are able to be out. I feared you were indisposed. Every one was saying, 'Miss Chantrey must be indisposed, as she was not at the funeral.' And I feared it was the case."

"No, thank you, I am quite well," said Elizabeth.

Miss Dobell seated herself, smoothing down her skirt. It was of a very bright blue, and she wore with it a little fawn-coloured jacket adorned with a black and white braid, which was arranged upon it in loops and spirals. She had on also a blue tie, fastened in a bow at her throat, and an extremely oddly-shaped hat, from one side of which depended a somewhat battered bunch of purple grapes. Beneath this rather bacchanalian headgear her old, mild straw-coloured face had all the effect of an anachronism.

"I am so glad to find you both. I am so glad to have the opportunity of explaining how it was that I did not attend the funeral. It was a great disappointment. Everything so impressive, by all accounts. Yes. But I could not have attended without proper mourning. No. Oh, no, it would have been impossible. Even though I was aware that poor dear Mr. Mottisfont entertained very singular ideas upon the subject of mourning, I know how much they grieved poor dear Agatha. They were very singular. I suppose, my dear, Elizabeth, that it is in deference to poor Mr. Mottisfont's wishes that you do not wear black. I said to every one at once—oh, at once—'depend upon it poor Mr. Mottisfont must have expressed a wish. Otherwise Miss Chantrey would certainly wear mourning— oh, certainly. After living so long in the house, and being like a daughter to him, it would be only proper, only right and proper.' That is what I said, and I am sure I was right. It was his wish, was it not?"

"He did not like to see people in black," said Elizabeth.

"No," said Miss Dobell in a flustered little voice. "Very strange, is it not? But then so many of poor Mr. Mottisfont's ideas were very strange. I cannot help remembering how they used to grieve poor dear Agatha. And his views—so sad—so very sad. But there, we must not speak of them now that he is dead. No. Doubtless he knows better now. Oh, yes, we must hope so. I do not know what made me speak of it. I should not have done so. No, not now that he is dead! It was not right, or charitable. But I really only intended to explain how it came about that I was not at the funeral. It was a great deprivation—a very great deprivation, but I was there in spirit—oh, yes, in spirit."

The purple grapes nodded a little in sympathy with Miss Dobell's nervous agitation. She put up a little hand, clothed in a brown woolen glove, and steadied them.

"I often think," she said, "that I should do well to purchase one black garment for such occasions as these. Now I should hardly have liked to come here to-day, dressed in colours, had I not been aware of poor dear Mr. Mottisfont's views. It is awkward. Yes, oh, yes. But you see, my dear Mary, in my youth, being one of a very large family, we were so continually in mourning that I really hardly ever possessed any garment of a coloured nature. When I was only six years old I can remember that we were in mourning for my grandfather. In those days, my dears, little girls, wore, well, they wore—little— hem—white trousers, quite long, you know, reaching in fact to the ankle. Under a black frock it had quite a garish appearance. And my dear mother, who was very particular about all family observances, used to stitch black crape bands upon the trouser-legs. It was quite a work. Oh, yes, I assure you. Then after my grandfather, there was my great-uncle George, and on the other side of the family my great-aunt Eliza. And then there were my uncles, and two aunts, and quite a number of cousins. And, later on, my own dear brothers and sisters. So that, as you may say, we were never out of black at all, for our means were such that it was necessary to wear out one garment before another could be purchased. And I became a little weary of wearing black, my dears. So when my last dear sister died, I went into colours. Not at once, oh, no!"—Miss Cobell became very much shocked and agitated at the sound of her own words. "Oh, dear, no. Not, of course, until after a full and proper period of mourning, but when that was over I went into colours, and have never since possessed anything black. You see, as I have no more relations, it is unnecessary that I should be provided with mourning."

Elizabeth Chantrey left her sister's house in rather a saddened mood. She wondered if she too would ever be left derelict. Unmarried women were often very lonely. Life went past them down other channels. They missed their link with the generations to come, and as the new life sprang up it knew them not, and they had neither part nor lot in it. When she reached home she sat for a long while very still, forcing her consciousness into a realisation of Life as a thing unbroken, one, eternal. The peace of it came upon her, and the sadness passed.

CHAPTER VI

THE LETTER

Oh, you shall walk in the mummers' train,
And dance for a beggar's boon,
And wear as mad a motley
As any under the moon,
And you shall pay the piper—
But I will call the tune.

OLD Mr. Mottisfont had been dead for about a fortnight when the letter arrived. David Blake found it upon his breakfast table when he came downstairs. It was a Friday morning, and there was an east wind blowing. David came into the dining-room wishing that there were no such thing as breakfast, and there, propped up in front of his plate, was the letter. He stared at it, and stared again. A series of sleepless or hag-ridden nights are not the best preparation for a letter written in a dead man's hand and sealed with a dead man's seal. If David's hand was steady when he picked up the letter it was because his will kept it steady, and for no other reason. As he held it in his hand, Mrs. Havergill came bustling in with toast and coffee. David passed her, went into his consulting room and shut the door.

"First he went red and then he went white," she told Sarah, "and he pushed past me as if I were a stock, or a post, or something of that sort. I 'ope he 'asn't caught one of them nasty fevers, down in some slum. 'Tisn't natural for a man to turn colour that way. There was only one young man ever I knew as did it, William Jones his name was, and he was the sexton's son down at Dunnington. And he'd do it. Red one minute and white the next, and then red again. And he went of in a galloping decline, and broke his poor mother's heart. And there's their two graves side by side in Dunnington Churchyard. Mr. Jones, he dug the graves hisself, and never rightly held his head up after."

David Blake sat down at his table and spread out old Mr. Mottisfont's letter upon the desk in front of him. It was a long letter, written in a clear, pointed handwriting, which was characteristic and unmistakable.

"My dear David,"—wrote old Mr. Mottisfont,—"My dear David, I have just written a letter to Edward—a blameless and beautiful letter—in which I have announced my immediate, or, as one might say, approximate intention of committing suicide by the simple expedient of first putting arsenic into a cup of tea and then drinking the tea. I shall send Edward for the tea, and I shall put the arsenic into it, under his very nose. And Edward will be thinking of beetles, and will not see me do it. I am prepared to bet my bottom dollar that he does not see me do it. Edward's letter, of which I enclose a copy, is the sort of letter which one shows to coroners, and jurymen, and legal advisers. Of course things may not have gone as far as that, but, on the other hand, they may. There are evil-minded persons who may have suspected Edward of having hastened my departure to a better world. You may even have suspected him yourself, in which case, of course, my dear David, this letter will be affording you a good deal of pleasurable relief." David clenched his hand and read on. "Edward's letter is for the coroner. It should arrive about a fortnight after my death, if my valued correspondent, William Giles, of New York, does as I have asked him. This letter is for you. Between ourselves, then, it was that possible three years of yours that decided me. I couldn't stand it. I don't believe in another world, and I 'm damned if I'll put in three years' hell in this one. Do you remember old Madden? I do, and I 'm not going to hang on like that, not to please any one, nor I 'm not going to be cut up in sections either. So now you know all about it. I've just sent Edward for the tea. Poor Edward, it will hurt his feelings very much to be suspected of polishing me off. By the way, David, as a sort of last word—you 're no end of a damn fool—why don't you marry the right woman instead of wasting your time hankering after the wrong one? That's all. Here's luck.

"Yours.
"E.M.M."

David read the letter straight through without any change of expression. When he came to the end he folded the sheets neatly, put them back in the envelope, and locked the envelope away in a drawer. Then his face changed suddenly. First, a great rush of colour came into it, and then every feature altered under an access of blind and ungovernable anger. He pushed back his chair and sprang up, but the impetus which had carried him to his feet appeared to receive some extraordinary check. His movement had been a very violent one, but all at once it passed into rigidity. He stood with every muscle tense, and made neither sound nor movement. Slowly the colour died out of his face. Then he took a step backwards and dropped again into the chair. His eyes were fixed upon the strip of carpet which lay between him and the writing-table. A small, twisted scrap of paper was lying there. David Blake looked hard at the paper, but he did not see it. What he saw was another torn and twisted thing.

A man's professional honour is a very delicate thing. David had never held his lightly. If he had violated it, he had done so because there were great things in the balance. Mary's happiness, Mary's future, Mary's life. He had betrayed a trust because Mary asked it of him and because there was so much in the balance. And it had all been illusion. There had been no risk—no danger. Nothing but an old man's last and cruelest dupe. A furious anger surged in him. For nothing, it was all for nothing. He had wrenched himself for nothing, forfeited his self-respect for nothing, sold his honour for nothing. Mary had bidden him, and he had done her bidding, and it was all for nothing. A little bleak sunlight came in at the window and showed the worn patches upon the carpet. David could remember that old brown carpet for as long as he could remember anything. It had been in his father's consulting room. The writing-table had been there too. The room was full of memories of William Blake. Old familiar words and looks came back to David as he sat there. He remembered many little things, and, as he remembered, he despised himself very bitterly. As the moments passed, so his self-contempt grew, until it became unbearable. He rose, pushing his chair so that it fell over with a crash, and went into the dining-room.

Half an hour later Sarah put her head round the corner of the door and announced, "Mr. Edward Mottisfont in the consulting room, sir." David Blake was sitting at the round table with a decanter in front of him. He got up with a short laugh and went to Edward.

Edward presented a ruffled but resigned appearance. He was agitated, but beneath the agitation there was plainly evident a trace of melancholy triumph.

"I've had a letter," he began. David stood facing him.

"So have I," he said.

Edward's wave of the hand dismissed as irrelevant all letters except his own. "But mine—mine was from my uncle," he exclaimed.

"Exactly. He was obliging enough to send me a copy."

"You—you know," said Edward. then he searched his pockets, and ultimately produced a folded letter.

"You've had a letter like this? He's told you? You know?"

"That he's played us the dirtiest trick on record? Yes, thanks, Edward, I've been enjoying the knowledge for the best part of an hour."

Edward shook his head.

"Of course he was mad," he said. "I have often wondered if he was quite responsible. He used to say such extraordinary things. If you remember, I asked you about it once, and you laughed at me. But now, of course, there is no doubt about it. His brain had become affected."

David's lip twitched a little.

"Mad? Oh, no, you needn't flatter yourself, he wasn't mad. I only hope my wits may last as well. He wasn't mad, but he's made the biggest fools of the lot of us—the biggest fools. Oh, Lord!—how he'd have laughed. He set the stage, and called the cast, and who so ready as we? First Murderer—Edward Mottisfont; Chief Mourner—Mary, his wife; and Tom Fool, beyond all other Tom Fools, David Blake, M.D. My Lord, he never said a truer word than when he wrote me down a damn fool!"

David ended on a note of concentrated bitterness, and Edward stared at him.

"I would much rather believe he was out of his mind," he said uncomfortably. "And he is dead—after all, he's dead."

"Yes," said David grimly, "he's dead."

"And thanks to you," continued Edward, "there has been no scandal—or publicity. It would really have been dreadful if it had all come out. Most—most unpleasant. I know you didn't wish me to say anything."

Edward began to rumple his hair wildly. "Mary told me, and of course I know it's beastly to be thanked, and all that, but I can't help saying that—in fact—I am awfully grateful. And I 'm awfully thankful that the matter has been cleared up so satisfactorily. If we hadn't got this letter, well—I don't like to say such a thing—but any one of us might have come to suspect the other. It doesn't sound quite right to say it," pursued Edward apologetically, "but it might have happened. You might have suspected me—oh, I don't mean really—I am only supposing, you know—or I might have suspected you. And now it's all cleared up, and no harm done, and as to my poor old uncle, he was mad. People who commit suicide are always mad. Every one knows that."

"Oh, have it your own way," said David Blake. "He was mad, and now everything is comfortably arranged, and we can all settle down with nothing on our minds, and live happily ever after."

There was a savage sarcasm in his voice, which he did not trouble to conceal.

"And now, look here," he went on with a sudden change of manner. He straightened himself and looked squarely at Edward Mottisfont. "Those letters have got to be kept."

"Now I should have thought—" began Edward, but David broke in almost violently.

"For Heaven's sake, don't start thinking, Edward." He said: "Just you listen to me. These letters have got to be kept. They've got to sit in a safe at a lawyer's. We'll seal 'em up in the presence of witnesses, and send 'em off. We 're not out of the wood yet. If this business were ever to leak out—and, after all, there are four of us in it, and two of them are women—if it were ever to leak out, we should want these letters to save our necks.

Yes—our necks. Good Lord, Edward, did you never realize your position? Did you never realize that any jury in the world would have hanged you on the evidence? It was damning—absolutely damning. And I come in as accessory after the fact. No, thank you, I think we'll keep the letters, until we 're past hanging. And there's another thing—how many people have you told? Mary, of course?"

"Yes, Mary, but no one else," said Edward.

David made an impatient movement.

"If you've told her, you've told her," he said. "Now what you've got to do is this: you've got to rub it into Mary that it's just as important for her to hold her tongue now as it was before the letter came. She was safe as long as she thought your neck was in danger, but do, for Heaven's sake, get it into her head that I 'm dead damned broke, if it ever gets out that I helped to hush up a case that looked like murder and turned out to be suicide. The law wouldn't hang me, but I should probably hang myself. I'd be broke. Rub that in."

"She may have told Elizabeth," said Edward hesitatingly. "I 'm afraid she may have told Elizabeth by now."

"Elizabeth doesn't talk," said David shortly.

"Nor does Mary." Edward's tone was rather aggrieved.

"Oh, no woman ever talks," said David.

He laughed harshly and Edward went away with his feelings of gratitude a little chilled, and a faint suspicion in his mind that David had been drinking.

CHAPTER VII

ELIZABETH CHANTREY

"Whatever ways we walk in and whatever dreams come true,
You still shall say, "God speed" to me, and I, "God go with you."

SOME days later Elizabeth Chantrey went away for about a month, to pay a few long-promised visits. She went first to an old school-friend, then to some relations, and lastly to the Mainwarings. Agneta Mainwaring had moved to town after her mother's death, and was sharing a small flat with her brother Louis, in a very fashionable quarter. She had been engaged for about six months to Douglas Strange, and was expecting to marry him as soon as he returned from his latest, and most hazardous journey across Equatorial Africa.

"I thought you were never coming," said Agneta, as they sat in the firelight, Louis on the farther side of the room, close to the lamp, with his head buried in a book.

"Never, never, *never!*" repeated Agneta, stroking the tail of Elizabeth's white gown affectionately and nodding at every word. She was sitting on the curly black hearth-rug, a small vivid creature in a crimson dress. Agneta Mainwaring was little and dark, passionate, earnest, and frivolous. A creature of variable moods and intense affections, steadfast only where she loved. Elizabeth was watching the firelight upon the big square sapphire ring which she always wore. She looked up from it now and smiled at Agneta, just a smile of the eyes.

"Well, I am here," she said, and Agneta went on stroking, and exclaimed:

"Oh, it's so good to have you."

"The world not been going nicely?" said Elizabeth.

Agneta frowned.

"Oh, so, so. Really, Lizabeth, being engaged to an explorer is the *devil*. Sometimes I get a letter two days running, and sometimes I don't get one for two months, and I've just been doing the two months' stretch."

"Then," said Elizabeth, "you'll soon be getting two letters together, Neta."

"Oh, well, I did get one this morning, or I shouldn't be talking about it," Agneta flushed and laughed, then frowned again. Three little wrinkles appeared upon her nose. "What worries me is that I am such a hopeless materialist about letters. Letters are rank materialism. Rank. Two people as much in touch with one another as Douglas and I oughtn't to need letters. I've no business to be dependent on them. We ought to be able to reach one another without them. Of course we do—*really*—but we ought to know that we are doing it. We ought to be conscious of it. I've no business to be dependent on wretched bits of paper, and miserable penfuls of ink. I ought to be able to do without them. And I 'm a blatant materialist. I can't."

Elizabeth laughed a little.

"I shouldn't worry, if I were you. It'll all come. You'll get past letters when you 're ready to get past them. I don't think your materialism is of a very heavy order. It will go away if you don't fuss over it. We'll all get past letters in time."

Agneta tossed her head.

"Oh, I don't suppose there'll be any letters in heaven," she said. "I 'm sure I trust not. My idea is that we shall sit on nice comfy clouds, and play at telephones with thought-waves."

Louis shut his book with a bang.

"Really, Agneta, if that isn't materialism." He came over and sat down on the hearth-rug beside his sister. They were not at all alike. Where Agneta was small, Louis was large. Her hair and eyes were black, and his of a dark reddish-brown.

"I didn't know you were listening," she said.

"Well, I wasn't. I just heard, and I give you fair warning, Agneta, that if there are going to be telephones in your heaven, I 'm going somewhere else. I shall have had enough of them here. Hear the bells, the silver bells, the tintinabulation that so musically swells. From the bells, bells, bells, bells—bells, bells, bells."

Agneta first pulled Louis's hair, and then put her fingers in her ears.

"Stop! stop this minute! Oh, Louis, please. Oh, Lizabeth, make him stop. That thing always drives me perfectly crazy, and he knows it."

"All right. It's done. I've finished. I 'm much more merciful than Poe. I only wanted to point out that if that was your idea of heaven, it wasn't mine."

"Oh, good gracious!" cried Agneta suddenly. She sprang up and darted to the door.

"What's the matter?"

"I've absolutely and entirely forgotten to order any food for to-morrow. Any food whatever. All right, Louis, you won't laugh when you have to lunch on bread and water, and Lizabeth takes the afternoon train back to her horrible Harford place, because we have starved her."

Louis gave a resigned sigh and leaned comfortably back against an empty chair. For some moments he gazed dreamily at Elizabeth. Then he said: "How nicely your hair shines. I like you all white and gold like that. If Browning had known you he needn't have written. 'What's become of all the gold, used to hang and brush their bosoms.' You've got your share."

"But my hair isn't golden at all, Louis," said Elizabeth.

Louis frowned.

"Yes, it is," he said, "it's gold without the dross—gold spiritualised. And you ought to know better than to pretend. You know as well as I do that your hair is a thing of beauty. The real joy for ever sort. It's no credit to you. You didn't make it. And you ought to be properly grateful for being allowed to walk about with a real live halo. Why should you pretend? If it wasn't pretence, you wouldn't take so much trouble about doing it. You'd just twist it up on a single hairpin."

"It wouldn't stay up," said Elizabeth.

"I wish it wouldn't. Oh, Lizabeth, won't you let it down just for once?"

"No, I won't," said Elizabeth, with pleasant firmness.

Louis fell into a gloom. His brown eyes darkened.

"I don't see why," he said; and Elizabeth laughed at him.

"Oh, Louis, will you ever grow up?"

Louis assumed an air of dignity. "My last book," he said, "was not only very well reviewed by competent and appreciative persons, but I would have you to know that it also brought me in quite a large and solid cheque. And my poems have had what is known as a *succèss d'estime*, which means that you and your publisher lose money, but the critics say nice things. These facts, my dear madam, all point to my having emerged from the nursery."

"Go on emerging, Louis," said Elizabeth, with a little nod of encouragement. Louis appeared to be plunged in thought. He frowned, made calculations upon his fingers, and finally inquired:

"How many times have I proposed to you, Lizabeth?"

Elizabeth looked at him with amusement.

"I really never counted. Do you want me to?"

"No. I think I've got it right. I think it must be eight times, because I know I began when I was twenty, and I don't think I've missed a year since. This," said Louis, getting on to his knees and coming nearer, "this will be number nine."

"Oh, Louis, don't," said Elizabeth.

"And why not?"

"Because it really isn't kind. Do you want me to go away to-morrow? If you propose to me, and I refuse you, every possible rule of propriety demands that I should immediately return to Market Harford. And I don't want to." Louis hesitated.

"How long are you staying?"

"Nice, hospitable young man. Agneta has asked me to stay for a fortnight."

"All right." Louis sat back upon his heels. "Let's talk about books. Have you read Pender's last? It's a wonder—just a wonder."

Elizabeth enjoyed her fortnight's stay very much. She was glad to be away from Market Harford, and she was glad to be with Agneta and Louis. She saw one or two good plays, had a great deal of talk of the kind she hade been starving for, and met a good many people who were doing interesting things. On the last day of her visit Agneta said:

"So you go back to Market Harford for a year. Is it because Mr. Mottisfont asked you to?"

"Partly."

There was a little pause.

"What are you going to do with your life, Lizabeth?"

Elizabeth looked steadily at the blue of her ring. Her eyes were very deep.

"I don't know, Neta. I 'm waiting to be told."

Agneta nodded, and looked understanding.

"And if you aren't told?"

"I think I shall be."

"But if not?"

"Well, that would be a telling in itself. If nothing happens before the year is up, I shall come up to London, and find some work. There's plenty."

"Yes," said Agneta. She put her little pointed chin in her hands and gazed at Elizabeth. There was something almost fierce in her eyes. She knew very little about David Blake, but she guessed a good deal more. And there were moments when it would have given her a great deal of pleasure to have spoken her mind on the subject.

They sat for a little while in silence, and then Louis came in, and wandered about the room until Agneta exclaimed at him:

"Do, for goodness' sake, sit down, Louis! You give me the fidgets."

Louis drifted over to the hearth. "Have you ordered any meals," he said, with apparent irrelevance.

"Tea, dinner, breakfast, lunch, tea, and dinner again." Agneta's tone was vicious. "Is that enough for you?"

"Very well, then, run away and write a letter to Douglas. I believe you are neglecting him, and there's a nice fire in the dining-room."

Agneta rose with outraged dignity. "I don't write my love-letters to order, thank you," she said "and you needn't worry about Douglas. If you want me to go away, I don't mind taking a book into the dining-room. Though, if you'll take my advice—but you won't—so I'll just leave you to find out for yourself."

Louis shut the door after her, and came back to Elizabeth.

"Number nine," he observed.

"No, Louis, don't."

"I 'm going to. You are in for it, Lizabeth. Your visit is over, so you can't accuse me of spoiling it. Number nine, and a fortnight overdue. Here goes. For the ninth time of asking, will you marry me?"

Elizabeth shook her head at him.

"No, Louis, I won't," she said.

Louis looked at her steadily.

"This is the ninth time I have asked you. How many times have you taken me seriously, Lizabeth? Not once."

"I should have been so very sorry to take you seriously, you see, Louis dear," said Elizabeth, speaking very sweetly and gently.

Louis Mainwaring walked to the window and stood there in silence for a minute or two. Elizabeth began to look troubled. When he turned round and came back his face was rather white.

"No," he said, "you've never taken me seriously—never once. But it's been serious enough, for me. You never thought it went deep—but it did. Some people hide their deep things under silence—every one can understand that. Others hide theirs under words—a great many light words. Jests. That's been my way. It's a better mask than the other, but I don't want any mask between us now. I want you to understand. We've always talked about my being in love with you. We've always laughed about it, but now I want you to understand. It's me, the whole of me—all there is—all there ever will be—"

He was stammering now and almost incoherent. His hand shook. Elizabeth got up quickly.

"Oh, Louis dear, Louis dear," she said. She put her arm half round him, and for a moment he leaned his head against her shoulder. When he raised it he was trying to smile.

"Oh, Lady of Consolation," he said, and then, "how you would spoil a man whom you loved! There, Lizabeth, you needn't worry about it. You see, I've always known that you would never love me."

"Oh, Louis, but I love you very much, only not just like that."

"Yes, I know. I've always known it and I've always known that there was some one else whom you did love—just like that. What I've been waiting for is to see it making you happy. And it doesn't make you happy. It never has. And, lately, there's been something fresh—something that has hurt. You've been very unhappy. As soon as you came here I knew. What is it? Can't you tell me?"

Elizabeth sat down again, but she did not turn her eyes away.

"No, Louis, I don't think I can." she said.

Louis's chin lifted.

"Does Agneta know?" he asked with a quick flash of jealously.

"No, she doesn't," said Elizabeth, reprovingly. "And she has never asked."

Louis laughed.

"That's for my conscience, I suppose," he said, "but I don't mind. I can bear it a lot better if you haven't told Agneta. And look here, Lizabeth, even if you never tell me a single word, I shall always know things about you—things that matter. I've always known when things went wrong with you, and I always shall."

It was obviously quite as an afterthought that he added:

"Do you mind?"

"No," said Elizabeth, slowly, "I don't think I mind. But don't look too close, Louis dear—not just now. It's kinder not to."

"All right," said Louis.

Then he came over and stood beside her. "Lizabeth, if there's anything I can do—any sort or kind of thing—you're to let me know. You will, won't you? You're the best thing in my world, and anything that I can do for you would be the best day's work I ever did. If you'll just clamp on to that we shall be all right."

Elizabeth looked up, but before she could speak, he bent down, kissed her hastily on the cheek, and went out of the room.

Elizabeth put her face in her hands and cried.

"I suppose Louis has been proposing to you again," was Agneta's rather cross comment. "Lizabeth, what on earth are you crying for?"

"Oh, Neta, do you hate me?" said Elizabeth in a very tired voice.

Agneta knelt down beside her, and began to pinch her arm.

"I would if I could, but I can't," she observed viciously. "I've tried, of course, but I can't do it by myself, and it's not the sort of thing you can expect religion to be any help in. As if you didn't know that Louis and I simply love your littlest finger-nail, and that we'd do anything for you, and that we think it an honour to be your friends, and—oh, Lizabeth, if you don't stop crying this very instant, I shall pour all the water out of that big flower-vase down the back of your neck!"

CHAPTER VIII

EDWARD SINGS

"What ails you, Andrew, my man's son,
  That you should look so white,
That you should neither eat by day,
  Nor take your rest by night?"

"I have no rest when I would sleep,
  No peace when I would rise,
Because of Janet's yellow hair,
  Because of Janet's eyes."

WHEN Elizabeth Chantrey returned to Market Harford, she did so with quite a clear understanding of the difficulties that lay before her. Edward had spoken to her of his uncle's wishes, and begged her to fulfill them by remaining on in the old house as his and Mary's guest. Apparently it never occurred to him that the situation presented any difficulty, or that few women would find it agreeable to be guest where they had been mistress. Elizabeth was under no illusions. She knew that she was putting herself in an almost impossible position, but she had made up her mind to occupy that position for a year. She had given David Blake so much already, that a little more did not seem to matter. Another year, a little more pain, were all in the day's work. She had given many years and had suffered much pain. Through the years, through the pain, there had been in the back of her mind the thought, "If he needed me, and I were not here." Elizabeth had always known that some day he would need her—not love her—but need her. And for that she waited.

Elizabeth returned to Market Harford on a fine November afternoon. The sun was shining, after two days' rain, and Elizabeth walked up from the station, leaving her luggage to the carrier. It was quite a short walk, but she met so many acquaintances that she was some time reaching home. First, it was old Dr. Bull with his square face and fringe of stiff grey beard who waved his knobbly stick at her, and waddled across the road. He was a great friend of Elizabeth's, and he greeted her warmly.

"Now, now, Miss Elizabeth, so you've not quite deserted us, hey? Glad to be back, hey?"

"Yes, very glad," said Elizabeth, smiling.

"And every one will be glad to see you, all your friends. Hey? I 'm glad, Edward and Mary'll be glad, and David—hey? David's a friend of yours, isn't he? Used to be, I know, in the old days. Prodigious allies you were. Always in each other's pockets. Same books—same walks—same measles—" he laughed heartily, and then broke off. "David wants his friends," he said, "for the matter of that, every one wants friends, hey? But you get David to come and see you, my dear. He won't want much persuading, hey? Well, well, I won't keep you. I mustn't waste your time. Now that I 'm idle, I forget that other people have business, hey? And I see Miss Dobell coming over to speak to you. Now, I wouldn't waste her time for the world. Not for the world, my dear Miss Elizabeth. Good-day, good-day, good-day."

His eyes twinkled as he raised his hat, and he went off at an astonishing rate, as Miss Dobell picked her way across the road.

"Such a fine man, Dr. Bull, I always think," she remarked in her precise little way. Every word she uttered had the effect of being enclosed in a separate little water-tight compartment. "I really miss him, if I may say so. Oh, yes; and I am not the only one of his old patients who feels it a deprivation to have lost his services. Oh, no. Young men are so unreliable. They begin well, but they are unreliable. Oh, yes, sadly unreliable," repeated Miss Dobell with emphasis.

She and Elizabeth were crossing the bridge as she spoke. Away to the left, above the water, Elizabeth could see the sunlight reflected from the long line of windows which faced the river. The trees before them were almost leafless, and it was easy to distinguish one house from another. David Blake lived in the seventh house, and Miss Dobell was gazing very pointedly in that direction, and nodding her head.

"I dislike gossip," she said. "I set my face against gossip, my dear Elizabeth, I do not approve of it. I do not talk scandal nor permit it to be talked in my presence. But I am not blind, or deaf. Oh, no. We should be thankful when we have all our faculties, and mine are unimpaired, oh, yes, quite unimpaired, although I am not quite as young as you are."

"Yes?" said Elizabeth.

Miss Dobell became rather flustered. ""I have a little errand," she said hurriedly. "A little errand, my dear Elizabeth. I will not keep you, oh, no, I must not keep you now. I shall see you later, I shall come and see you, but I will not detain you now. Oh, no, Mary will be waiting for you."

"So you have really come," said Mary a little later.

After kissing her sister warmly, she had allowed a slight air of offence to appear. "I had begun to think you had missed your train. I am afraid the tea will be rather strong, I had it made punctually, you see. I was beginning to think that you hadn't been able to tear yourself away from Agneta after all."

"Now, Molly—" said Elizabeth, protestingly.

But Mary was not to be turned aside. "Of course you would much rather have stayed, I know that. Will you have bread and butter or tea-cake? When Mr. Mottisfont died, I said to myself, 'Now she'll go and live with Agneta, and she might just as well be *dead*.' That's why I was quite pleased when Edward came and told me that Mr. Mottisfont had said you were to stay on here for a year. Of course, as I said to Edward, if it had been any one but you, I shouldn't have liked it at all. That's what I said to Edward—'It really isn't fair, but Elizabeth isn't like other people. She won't try and run the house over my head, and she won't want to be always with us.' You see, married people do like to have their evenings, but as I said to Edward, 'Elizabeth would much rather be in her own little room, with a book, than sitting with us.' And you would, wouldn't you?"

"Oh, yes," said Elizabeth laughing.

The spectacle of Mary being tactful always made her laugh.

"Of course when any one comes in the evening—that's different. Of course you'll join us then. But you'd rather be here as a rule, wouldn't you?"

"Oh, you know I love my little room. It was nice of you to have tea here, Molly," said Elizabeth.

"Yes, I thought you'd like it. And then I wanted the rest of the house to be a surprise to you. When we've had tea I want to show you everything. Of course your rooms haven't been touched, you said you'd rather they weren't; but everything else has been done up, and I really think it's very nice. I've been quite excited over it."

"Give me a little more tea, Molly," said Elizabeth.

As she leaned forward with her cup in her hand, she asked casually: "Have you seen much of David lately?"

"Oh, yes," said Mary, "he's here very often." She pursed her lips a little. "I think David is a *very* curious person, Liz. I don't understand him at all. I think he is very difficult to understand."

"Is he, Molly?"

Elizabeth looked at her sister with something between anxiety and amusement.

"Yes, very. He's quite changed, it seems to me. I could understand his being upset just after Mr. Mottisfont's death. We were all upset then. I am sure I never felt so dreadful in my life. It made me quite ill. But afterwards," Mary's voice dropped to a lower tone, "afterwards when the letter had come, and everything was cleared up—well, you'd have thought he would have been all right again, wouldn't you? And instead, he has just gone on getting more and more unlike himself. You know, he was so odd when Edward went to see him that, really,"—Mary hesitated—"Edward thought—well, he wondered whether David had been drinking."

"Nonsense, Molly!"

"Oh, it's not only Edward—everybody has noticed how changed he is. Have you got anything to eat, Liz? Have some of the iced cake; it's from a recipe of Miss Dobell's and it's quite nice. What was I saying? Oh, about David—well, it's true, Liz—Mrs. Havergill told Markham; now, Liz, what's the sense of your looking at me like that? Of *course* I shouldn't *dream* of talking to an ordinary servant, but considering Markham has known us since we were about two—Markham takes an interest, a real interest, and when Mrs. Havergill told her that she was afraid David was taking a great deal more than was good for him, and she wished his friends could stop it, why, Markham naturally told me. She felt it her duty. I expect she thought I might have an *influence*—as I hope I have. That's why I encourage David to come here. I think it's so good for him. I think it makes such a difference to young men if they have a nice home to come to, and it's very good for them to see married people fond of each other, and happy together, like Edward and I are. Don't you think so?"

"I don't know, Molly," said Elizabeth. "Are people talking about David?"

"Yes, they are. Of course I haven't said a word, but people are noticing how different he is. I don't see how they can help it, and yesterday when I was having tea with Mrs. Codrington, Miss Dobell began to hint all sorts of things, and there was quite a scene. You know how devoted Mrs. Codrington is! She really quite frightened poor little Miss Hester. I can tell you, I was glad that I hadn't said anything. Mrs. Codrington always frightens me. She looks so large, and she speaks so loud. I was quite glad to get away."

"I like Mrs. Codrington," said Elizabeth.

"Oh, well, so do I. But I like her better when she's not angry. Oh, by the way, Liz, talking of David, do you know that I met Katie Ellerton yesterday, and—how long is it since Dr. Ellerton died?"

"More than two years."

"Well, she has gone quite out of mourning. You know how she went on at first—she was going to wear weeds always, and never change anything, and as to ever going into colours again, she couldn't imagine how any one could do it! And I met her out yesterday in quite a bright blue coat and skirt. What do you think of that?"

"Oh, Molly, you've been going out to too many tea-parties! Why shouldn't poor Katie go out of mourning? I think it's very sensible of her. I have always been so sorry for her."

Mary assumed an air of lofty virtue. "I *used* to be. But now, I don't approve of her at all. She's just doing her very best to catch David Blake. Every one can see it. If that wretched little Ronnie has so much as a thorn in his finger, she sends for David. She's making herself the laughing-stock of the place. I think it's simply horrid. I don't approve of second marriages at all. I never do see how any really nice-minded woman can marry again. And it's not only the marrying, but to run after a man, like that—it's quite dreadful! I am sure David would be most unhappy if he married her. It would be a dreadfully bad thing for him."

Elizabeth leaned back in her chair.

"How sweet the hour that sets us free
To sip our scandal, and our tea,"

she observed.

Mary coloured.

"I never talk scandal," she said in an offended voice, and Elizabeth refrained from telling her that Miss Dobell had made the same remark.

All the time that Mary was showing her over the house, Elizabeth was wondering whether it would be such a dreadfully bad thing for David to marry Katie Ellerton. Ronnie was a dear little boy, and David loved children, and Katie—Katie was one of those gentle, clinging creatures whom men adore and spoil. If she cared for him, and he grew to care for her—Elizabeth turned the possibilities over and over in her mind, wondering—

She wondered still more that evening, when David Blake came in after dinner. He had changed. Elizabeth looked at him and saw things in his face which she only half understood. He looked ill and tired, but both illness and weariness appeared to here to be incidental. Behind them there was something else, something much stronger and yet more subtle, some deflection of the man's whole nature.

Edward and Mary did not disturb themselves at David's coming. They were at the piano, and Edward nodded casually, whilst Mary merely waved her hand and smiled.

David said "How do you do?" to Elizabeth, and sat down by the fire. He was in evening dress, but somehow he looked out of place in Mary's new white drawing-room. Edward had put in electric light all over the house, and here it shone through rosy shades. The room was all rose and white—roses on the chintz, a frieze of roses upon the walls, and a rose-coloured carpet on the floor. Only the two lamps over the piano were lighted. They shone on Mary. She was playing softly impassioned chords in support of Edward, who exercised a pleasant tenor voice upon the lays of Lord Henry Somerset. Mary played accompaniments with much sentiment. Occasionally, when the music was easy, she shot an adoring glance at Edward, a glance to which he duly responded, when not preoccupied with a note beyond his compass.

Elizabeth was tolerant of lovers, and Mary's little sentimentalities, like Mary's airs of virtuous matronhood, were often quite amusing to watch; but to-night, with David Blake as a fourth person in the room, Elizabeth found amusement merging into irritation and irritation into pain. Except for that lighted circle about the piano, the room lay all in shadow. There was a soft dusk upon it, broken every now that then by gleams of firelight.

David Blake sat back in his chair, and the dimness of the room hid his face, except when the fire blazed up and showed Elizabeth how changed it was. She had been away only a month, and he looked like a stranger. His attitude was that of a very weary man. His head rested on his hand, and he looked all the time at Mary in the rosy glow which bathed her. When she looked up at Edward, he saw the look, saw the light shine down into her dark eyes and sparkle there. Not a look, not a smile was lost, and whilst he watched Mary, Elizabeth watched him. Elizabeth was very glad of the dimness that shielded her. It was a relief to drop the mask of a friendly indifference, to be able to watch David with no thought except for him. Her heart yearned to him as never before. She divined in him a great hunger—a great pain. And this hunger, this pain, was hers. The longing to give, to assuage, to comfort, welled up in her with a suddenness and strength that were almost startling. Elizabeth took her thought in a strong hand, forcing it along accustomed channels from the plane where love may be thwarted, to that other plane, where love walks unashamed and undeterred, and gives her gifts, no man forbidding her. Elizabeth sat still, with folded hands. Her love went out to David, like one ripple in a boundless, golden sea, from which they drew their being, and in which they lived and moved. A sense of light and peace came down upon her.

Edward's voice was filling the room. It was quite a pleasant voice, and if it never varied into expression, at least it never went out of tune, and every word was distinct.

"Ah, well, I know the sadness
   That tears and rends your heart,
How that from all life's gladness
   You stand, far, far apart—"

sang Edward, in tones of the most complete unconcern.

It was Mary who supplied all the sentiment that could be wished for. She dwelt on the chords with an almost superfluous degree of feeling, and her eyes were quite moist.

At any other time this combination of Edward and Lord Henry Somerset would have entertained Elizabeth not a little, but just now there was no room in her thoughts for any one but David. The light that was upon her gave her vision. She looked upon David with eyes that had grown very clear, and as she looked she understood. That he had changed, deteriorated, she had seen at the first glance. Now she discerned in him the cause of such an alteration—something wrenched and twisted. The scene in her little brown room rose vividly before her. When David had allowed Mary to sway him, he had parted with something, which he could not now recall. He had broken violently through his own code, and the broken thing was failing him at every turn. Mary's eyes, Mary's voice, Mary's touch—these things had waked in him something beyond the old passion. The emotional strain of that scene had carried him beyond his self-control. A feverish craving was upon him, and his whole nature burned in the flame of it.

Edward had passed to another song.

"One more kiss from my darling one," he sang in a slightly perfunctory manner. His voice was getting tired, and he seemed a little absent-minded for a lover who was about to plunge into Eternity. The manner in which he requested death to come speedily was a trifle unconvincing. As he began the next verse David made a sudden movement. A log of wood upon the fire had fallen sharply, and there was a quick upward rush of flame. David looked round, facing the glow, and as he did so his eyes met Elizabeth's. Just for one infinitesimal moment something seemed to pass from her to him. It was one of those strange moments which are not moments of time at all, and are therefore not subject to time's laws. Elizabeth Chantrey's eyes were full of peace. Full, too, of a passionate gentleness. It was a gentleness which for an instant touched the sore places in David's soul with healing, and for that one instant David had a glimpse of something very strong, very tender, that was his, and yet incomprehensibly withheld from his understanding. It was one of those instantaneous flashes of thought—one of those gleams of recognition which break upon the dullness of material sense. Before and after—darkness, the void, the unstarred night, a chaos of things forgotten. But for one dazzled instant, the lightning stab of Truth, unrealized.

Elizabeth did not look away, or change colour. The peace was upon her still. She smiled a little, and as the moment passed, and the dark closed in again upon David's mind, she saw a spark of rather savage humour come into his eyes.

"Then come Eternity—"

"No, that's enough, Mary, I 'm absolutely hoarse," remarked Edward, all in the same breath, and with very much the same expression.

Mary got up, and began to shut the piano. The light shone on her white, uncovered neck.

CHAPTER IX

MARY IS SHOCKED

Through fire and frost and snow
   I see you go,
I see your feet that bleed,
   My heart bleeds too.
I, who would give my very soul for you,
   What can I do?
I cannot help your need.

THAT first evening was one of many others, all on very much the same pattern. David Blake would come in, after tea, or after dinner, sit for an hour in almost total silence, and then go away again. Every time that he came, Elizabeth's heart sank a little lower. This change, this obscuring of the man she loved, was an unreality, but how some unrealities have power to hurt us.

December brought extra work to the Market Harford doctors. There was an epidemic of measles amongst the children, combined with one of influenza amongst their elders. David Blake stood the extra strain but ill. He was slipping steadily down the hill. His day's work followed only too often upon a broken or sleepless night, and to get through what had to be done, or to secure some measure of sleep, he had recourse more and more frequently to stimulant. If no patient of his ever saw him the worse for drink, he was none the less constantly under its influence. If it did not intoxicate him, he came to rely upon its stimulus, and to distrust his unaided strength. He could no longer count upon his nerve, and the fear of all that nerve failure may involve haunted him continually and drove him down.

"Look here, Blake, you want a change. Why don't you go away?" said Tom Skeffington. It was a late January evening, and he had dropped in for a smoke and a chat. "The press of work is over now, and I could very well manage the lot for a fortnight or three weeks. Will you go?"

"No, I won't," said David shortly.

Young Skeffington paused. It was not much after six in the evening, and David's face was flushed, his hand unsteady.

"Look here, Blake," he said, and then stopped, because David was staring at him out of eyes that had suddenly grown suspicious.

"Well?" said David, still staring.

"Well, I should go away if I were you—go to Switzerland, do some winter sports. Get a thorough change. Come back yourself again."

There was ever so slight an emphasis on the last few words, and David flashed into sudden anger.

"Mind your own business, and be damned to you, Skeffington," he cried.

Tom Skeffington shrugged his shoulders.

"Oh, certainly," he said, and made haste to be gone.

Blake in this mood was quite impracticable. He had no mind for a scene.

David sat on, with a tumbler at his elbow. So they wanted him out of the way. That was the third person who had told him he needed a change—the third in one week.

Edward was one, and old Dr. Bull, and now Skeffington. Yes, of course, Skeffington would like him out of the way, so as to get all the practice into his own hands. Edward too. Was it this morning, or yesterday morning, that Edward had asked him when he was going to take a holiday? Now he came to think of it, it was yesterday morning. And he supposed that Edward wanted him out of the way too. Perhaps he went too often to Edward's house. David began to get angry. Edward was an ungrateful hound. "Damned ungrateful," said David's muddled brain. The idea of going to see Mary began to present itself to him. If Edward did not like it, Edward could lump it. He had been told to come whenever he liked. Very well, he liked now. Why shouldn't he?

He got up and went out into the cold. Then, when he was half-way up the High Street he remembered that Edward had gone away for a couple of days. It occurred to him as a very agreeable circumstance. Mary would be alone, and they would have a pleasant, friendly time together. Mary would sit in the rosy light and play to him, not to Edward, and sing in that small sweet voice of hers—not to Edward, but to him.

It was a cold, crisp night, and the frosty air heightened the effect of the stimulant which he had taken. He had left his own house flushed, irritable, and warm, but he arrived at the Mottisfonts' as unmistakably drunk as a man may be who is still upon his legs.

He rushed past Markham in the hall before she had time to do more than notice that his manner was rather odd, and she called after him that Mrs. Mottisfont was in the drawing-room.

David went up the stairs walking quite steadily, but his brain, under the influence of one idea, appeared to work in a manner entirely divorced from any volition of his.

Mary was sitting before the fire, in the rosy glow of his imagining. She wore a dim purple gown, with a border of soft dark fur. A book lay upon her lap, but she was not reading. Her head, with its dark curls, rested against the rose-patterned chintz of the chair. Her skin was as white as a white rose leaf. Her lips as softly red as real red roses. A little amethyst heart hung low upon her bosom and caught the light. There was a bunch of violets at her waist. The room was sweet with them.

Mary looked up half startled as David Blake came in. He shut the door behind him, with a push, and she was startled outright when she saw his face. He looked at her with glazed eyes, and smiled a meaningless and foolish smile.

"Edward is out," said Mary, "he is away." And then she wished that she had said anything else. She looked at the bell, and wondered where Elizabeth was. Elizabeth had said something about going out—one of her sick people.

"Yes—out," said David, still smiling. "That's why I've come. He's out—Edward's out—gone away. You'll play to me—not to Edward—to-night. You'll sit in this nice pink light and—play to me, won't you—Mary dear?" The words slipped into one another, tripped, jostled, and came with a run.

David advanced across the room, moving with caution, and putting each foot down slowly and carefully. His irritability had vanished. He felt instead a pleasant sense of warmth and satisfaction. He let himself sink into a chair and gazed at Mary.

"Le's sit down—and have nice long talk," he said in an odd, thick voice; "we haven't had—nice long talk—for months. Le's talk now."

Mary began to tremble. Except in the streets, she had never seen a man drunk before, and even in the streets, passing by on the other side of the road, under safe protection, and with head averted, she had felt sick and terrified. What she felt now she hardly knew. She looked at the bell. She would have to pass quite close to David before she could reach it.

Elizabeth—she might ring and ask if Elizabeth had come in. Yes, she might do that. She made a step forward, but as she reached to touch the bell, David leaned sideways, with a sudden heavy jerk, and caught her by the wrist.

"What's that for?" he asked.

Suspicion roused in him again, and he frowned as he spoke. His face was very red, and his eyes looked black. Mary had cried out, when he caught her wrist. Now, as he continued to hold it, she stared at him in helpless silence. Then quite suddenly she burst into hysterical tears.

"Let me go—oh, let me go! Go away, you 're not fit to be here! You 're drunk. Let me go at once! How dare you?"

David continued to hold her wrist, not of any set purpose, but stupidly. He seemed to have forgotten to let it go. The heat and pressure of his hand, his slow vacant stare, terrified Mary out of all self-control. She tried to pull her hand away, and as David's clasp tightened, and she felt her own helplessness, she screamed aloud, and almost as she did so the door opened sharply and Elizabeth Chantrey came into the room. She wore a long green coat, and dark furs, and her colour was bright and clear with exercise. For one startled second she stood just inside the room, with her hand upon the door. Then, as she made a step forward, David relaxed his grasp, and Mary, wrenching her hand away, ran sobbing to meet her sister.

"Oh, Liz! Oh, Liz!" she cried.

Elizabeth was cold to the very heart. David's face—the heavy, animal look upon it—and Mary's frightened pallor, the terror in he eyes. What had happened?

She caught Mary by the arm.

"What is it?"

"He held me—he wouldn't let me go. He caught my wrist when I was going to ring the bell, and held it. Make him go away, Liz."

Elizabeth drew a long breath of relief. She scarcely knew what she had feared, but she felt suddenly as if an intolerable weight had been lifted from her mind. The removal of this weight set her free to think and act.

"Molly, hush! Do you hear me, hush! Pull yourself together! Do you know I heard you scream half-way up the stairs? Do you want the servants to hear too?"

She spoke in low, rapid tones, and Mary caught her breath like a child.

"But he's tipsy, Liz. Oh, Liz, make him go away," she whispered.

David had got upon his feet. He was looking at the two women with a puzzled frown.

"What's the matter?" he said slowly, and Mary turned on him with a sudden spurt of temper.

"I wonder you 're not ashamed," she said in rather a trembling voice. "I do wonder you 're not—and will you please go away at once, or do you want the servants to come in, and every one to know how disgracefully you have behaved?"

"Molly, hush!" said Elizabeth again.

Her own colour died away, leaving her very pale. Her eyes were fixed on David with a look between pity and appeal. She left Mary and went to him.

"David," she said, putting her hand on his arm, "won't you go home now? It's getting late. It's nearly dinner time, and I 'm afraid we can't ask you to stay to-night."

Something in her manner sobered David a little. Mary had screamed—why? What had he said to her—or done? She was angry. Why? Why did Elizabeth look at him like that? His mind was very much confused. Amid the confusion an idea presented itself to him. They thought that he was drunk. Well, he would show them, he would show them that he was not drunk. He stood for a moment endeavouring to bring the confusion of his brain into something like order. Then without a word he walked past Mary, and out of the room, walking quite steadily because a sober man walks steadily and he had to show them that he was sober.

Mary stood by the door listening. "Liz," she whispered, "he hasn't gone down-stairs." Her terror returned. "Oh, what is he doing? He has gone down the passage to Edward's room. Oh, do you think he's safe? Liz, ring the bell—do ring the bell."

Elizabeth shook her head. She came forward and put her hand on Mary's shoulder.

"No, Molly, it's all right," she said. She, too, listened, but Mary broke in on the silence with half a sob.

"You don't know how he frightened me. You don't know how dreadful he was—like a great stupid animal. Oh, I don't know how he dared to come to me like that. And my wrist aches still, it does, indeed. Oh! Liz, he's coming back."

They heard his steps coming along the passage, heavy, deliberate steps. Mary moved quickly away from the door, but Elizabeth stood still, and David Blake touched her dress as he came back into the room and shut the door behind him. His hair was wet from a liberal application of cold water. His face was less flushed and his eyes had lost the vacant look. He was obviously making a very great effort, and as obviously Mary had no intention of responding to it. She stood and looked at him, and ceased to be afraid. This was not the stranger who had frightened her. This was David Blake again, the man whom she could play upon, and control. The fright in her eyes gave place to a dancing spark of anger.

"I thought I asked you to go away," she said, and David winced at the coldness of her voice.

"Will you please go?"

"Mary—"

"If you want to apologise you can do so later—when you are fit," said Mary, her brows arched over very scornful eyes.

David was still making a great effort at self-control. He had turned quite white, and his eyes had rather a dazed look.

"Mary, don't," he said, and there was so much pain in his voice that Elizabeth made a half step towards him, and then stopped, because it was not any comfort of hers that he desired.

Mary's temper was up, and she was not to be checked. She meant to have her say, and if it hurt David, why, so much the better. He had given her a most dreadful fright, and he deserved to be hurt. It would be very good for him. Anger reinforced by a high moral motive is indeed a potent weapon. Mary wielded it unmercifully.

"Don't—don't," she said. "Oh, of course not. You behave disgracefully—you take advantage of Edward's being away—you come here drunk—and I 'm not to say a word—"

Her eyes sparkled, and her head was high. She gave a little angry laugh, and turned towards the bell.

"Will you go, please, or must I ring for Markham?"

At her movement, and the sound of her laughter, David's self-control gave way, suddenly and completely. The blood rushed violently to his head. He took a long step towards her, and she stopped where she was in sheer terror.

"You laugh," he said, in a low tone of concentrated passion—"you laugh—"

Then his voice leaped into fury. "I've sold my soul for you, and you laugh. I 'm in hell for you, and you laugh. I 'm drunk, and you laugh. My God, for that at least you shall never laugh at me again. By God, you shan't—"

He stood over her for a moment, looking down on her with terrible eyes. Then he turned and went stumbling to the door, and so out, and, in the dead silence that followed, they heard the heavy front door swing to behind him.

Mary was clinging to a chair.

"Oh, Liz," she whispered faintly, but Elizabeth turned and went out of the room without a single word.

CHAPTER X

EDWARD IS PUT OUT

That which the frost can freeze,
  That which is burned of the fire,
Cast it down, it is nothing worth
  In the ways of the Heart's Desire.

Foot or hand that offends,
  Eye that shrinks from the goal,
Cast them forth, they are nothing worth,
  And fare with the naked soul.

MARY did not tell Edward about the scene with David Blake.

"You know, Liz, he behaved shamefully, but I don't want there to be a quarrel with Edward, and it would be sure to make a quarrel. And then people would talk, and there's no knowing what they would say. I think it would be perfectly dreadful to be talked about. I 'm sure I can't think how Katie Ellerton can stand it. Really, every one is talking about her."

In her heart of hearts Mary was a little flattered at David's last outburst. She would not for the world have admitted that this was the case, but it certainly contributed to her resolution not to tell Edward.

"I suppose some people would never forgive him," she said to Elizabeth, "but I don't think that's right, do you? I don't think it's at all Christian. I don't think one ought to be hard. He might do something desperate. I saw him go into Katie Ellerton's only this morning. I think I'll write him a little note, not referring to anything of course, and ask him if he won't come in to supper on Sundays. Then he'll see that I mean to forgive him, and there won't be any more fuss."

Sunday appeared to be quite a suitable day upon which to resume the role of guardian angel. Mary felt a pleasant glow of virtue as she wrote her little note and sent it off to David.

David Blake did not accept either the invitation or the olive branch. His anger against Mary was still stronger than his craving for her presence. He wrote a polite excuse and sat all that evening with his eyes fixed upon a book, which he made no pretence of reading. He had more devils than one to contend with just now. David had a strong will, and he was putting the whole strength of it into fighting the other craving, the craving for drink. In his sudden heat of passion he had taken an oath that he meant to keep. He had been drunk, and Mary had laughed at him. Neither Mary nor any one else should have that cause for mocking laughter again, and he sat nightly with a decanter at his elbow.

"And," as Mrs. Havergill remarked, "never touching a mortal drop," because if he was to down the devil at all he meant to down him in a set battle, and not to spend his days in ignominious flight.

Mrs. Havergill prognosticated woe to Sarah, with a mournful zest.

"Them sudden changes isn't 'olesome, and I don't hold with them, Sarah, my girl. One young man I knew, Maudsley 'is name was, he got the 'orrors, and died a-raving. And all through being cut off his drink too sudden. He broke 'is leg, and 'is mother, she said, 'Now I'll break 'im of the drink.' A very strict Methody woman, were Jane Ann Maudsley. 'Now I'll break 'im' sayd she; and there she sits and watches 'im, and the pore feller 'ollering for whisky, just fair 'ollering. 'Gemme a drop, Mother,' says he. 'Not I,' says she. 'It's 'ell fire, William,' says she. 'I'm all on fire now, Mother,' says he. 'Better burn now than in 'ell, William,' says Jane Ann; and then the 'orrors took him, and he died. A fine, proper young man as ever stepped, and very sweet on me before I took up with Havergill," concluded Mrs. Havergill meditatively, whilst Sarah shivered, and wished, as she afterwards confessed to a friend, "that Mrs. Havergill would be more cheerful like—just once in a way, for a change, as it were."

"For she do fair give a girl the 'ump sometimes," concluded Sarah, after what was for her quite a long speech.

Mrs. Havergill was a very buxom and comely person of unimpeachable respectability, but her fund of doleful reminiscence had depressed more than Sarah. David had been known to complain of it between jest and earnest. On one such occasion, at a tea-party to which Mary Chantrey had inveigled him, Miss Dobell ventured a mild protest.

"But she is such a treasure. Oh, yes. Your dear mother always found her so."

David winced a little. His mother had not been dead very long then. He regarded Miss Dobell with gravity.

"I have always wondered," he said, "whether it was an early apprenticeship to a ghoul which has imparted such a mortuary turn to Mrs. Havergill's conversation, or whether it is due to the fact of her having a few drops of Harvey's Sauce in her veins."

"Harvey's Sauce?" inquired the bewildered Miss Dobell.

David explained in his best professional manner.

"I said Harvey's Sauce because it is an old and cherished belief of mind that the same talented gentleman invented the sauce and composed the well-known 'Meditations among the Tombs.' The only point upon which I feel some uncertainty is this: Did he compose the Meditations because the sauce had disagreed with him, or did he invent the sauce as a sort of cheerful antidote to the Meditations? Now which do you suppose, Miss Dobell?"

Miss Dobell became very much fluttered.

"Oh, I 'm afraid—" she began. "I really had no idea that Harvey's Sauce was an unwholesome condiment. Yes, indeed, I fear that I cannot be of any great assistance, or in fact of any assistance at all. No, oh, no. I fear, Dr. Blake, that you must ask some one else who is better informed than myself. Oh, yes."

Afterwards she confided to Mary Chantrey that she had never heard of the work in question. "Have you, my dear?"

"No, never," said Mary, who was not greatly attracted by the title. Girls of two-and-twenty with a disposition to meditate among the tombs are mercifully rare.

"But," pursued little Miss Dobell with a virtuous lift of the chin, "the title has a religious sound—yes, quite a religious sound. I hope, oh, yes, indeed, I hope that Dr. Blake has no dreadful skeptical opinions. They are so very shocking," and Mary said, "Yes, they are, and I hope not, too." Even in those days she was a little inclined to play at being David's guardian angel.

Those days were two years old now. Sometimes it seemed to David that they belonged to another life.

Meanwhile he had his devil to fight. In the days that followed he fought the devil, and beat him, but without either pride or pleasure in the victory, for, deprived of stimulant, he fell again into the black pit of depression. Insomnia stood by his pillow and made the nights longer and more dreadful than the longest, gloomiest day.

Mary met him in the High Street one day, and was really shocked at his looks. She reproached. herself for neglecting him, smiled upon him sweetly, and said:

"Oh, David, do come and see us. Edward will be so pleased. He got a parcel of butterflies from Java last week, and he would so much like you to see them. He was saying so only this morning."

David made a suitable response. His anger was gone. Mary was Mary. If she were unkind, she was still Mary. If she were trivial, foolish, cruel, what did it matter? Her voice made his blood leap, her eyes were like wine, her hand played on his pulses, and he asked nothing more than to feel that soft touch, and answer to it, with every high-strung nerve. He despised her a little, and himself a good deal, and when a man's passion for a woman is mingled with contempt, it goes but ill with his soul.

That evening saw him again in his old place. He came and went as of old, and, as of old, his fever burned, and burning, fretted away both health and self-respect. He slept less and less, and if sleep came at all, it was so thin, so haunted by ill dreams, that waking was a positive relief. At least when he waked he was still sane, but in those dreams there lurked an impending horror that might at any moment burst the gloom, and stare him mad. It was madness that he feared in the days which linked that endless processing of long, unendurable nights. It was about this time that he began to be haunted by a strange vision, which, like the impending terror, lay just beyond the bounds of consciousness. As on the one side madness lurked, so on the other there were hints, stray gleams, as it were, from some place of peace. And the strange thing about it was, that at these moments a conviction would seize him that this place was his by right. His the deep waters of comfort, and his the wide, unbroken fields of peace, his—but lost.

Yet during all this time David went about his work, and if his patients thought him looking ill, they had no reason to complain either of inefficiency or neglect. His work was in itself a stimulant to him, a stimulant which braced his nerves and cleared his brain during the time that he was under its influence, and then resulted, like all stimulants, in a reaction of fatigue and nervous strain.

In the first days of March, Elizabeth Chantrey had a visit from old Dr. Bull. He sat and had tea with her in her little brown room, and talked about the mild spring weather and the show of buds upon the apple tree in his small square of garden. He also told her that Mrs. Codrington had three broods of chickens out, a fact of which Elizabeth had already been informed by Mrs. Codrington herself. When Dr. Bull had finished dealing with the early chickens, he asked for another cup of tea, took a good pull at it, wiped his square beard with a very brilliant pocket-handkerchief in which the prevailing colours were sky-blue and orange, and remarked abruptly:

"Why don't you get David Blake to go away, hey?—hey?"

Elizabeth frowned a little. This was getting to close quarters.

"I?" she said, with a note of gentle surprise in her voice.

Dr. Bull was quite ready for her. "You is the second person plural—or used to be when I went to school. You, and Mary, and Edward, you 're his friends, aren't you?—and two of you are women, so he'll have to be polite, hey? Can't bite your heads off the way he bit off mine, when I suggested that a holiday 'ud do him good. And he wants a holiday, hey?"

Elizabeth nodded.

"He ought to go away," she said.

"He'll break down if he doesn't," said Dr. Bull. He finished his cup of tea, and held it out. "Yes, another, please. You make him go, and he'll come back a new man. What's the good of being a woman if you can't manage a man for his good?"

Elizabeth thought the matter over for an hour, and then she spoke to Edward.

"He won't go," said Edward, with a good deal of irritation. "I asked him some little time ago whether he wasn't going to take a holiday. Now what is there in that to put any one's back up? And yet, I do assure you, he looked at me as if I had insulted him. Really, Elizabeth, I can't make out what has happened to David. He never used to be like this. And he comes here too often, a great deal too often. I shall have to tell him so, and then there'll be a row, and I simply hate rows. But really, a man in his state, always under one's feet—it gets on one's nerves."

"Edward is getting dreadfully put out," said Mary the same evening. She had come down to Elizabeth's room to borrow a book, and lingered for a moment or two, standing by the fire and holding one foot to the blaze. It was a night of sudden frost after the mild spring day.

"How cold it has turned," said Mary. "Yes, I really don't know what to do. If Edward goes on being tiresome and jealous"—she bridled a little as she spoke—"if he goes on—well, David will just have to stay away, and I 'm afraid he will feel it. I am afraid it may be bad for him. You know I have always hoped that I was being of some use to David—I have always wanted to have an influence—a good influence does make such a difference, doesn't it? I've never flirted with David—I really haven't—you know that, Liz?"

"No," said Elizabeth slowly. "You haven't flirted with him, Molly, my dear, but I think you are in rather a difficult position for being a good influence. You see, David is in love with you, and I think it would be better for him if he didn't see you quite so often."

Mary's colour rose.

"I can't help his being—fond of me," she said, with a slight air of offended virtue. "I am sure I don't know what you mean by my not being good for him. If it weren't for me he might be drinking himself to death at this very moment. You know how he was going on, and I am sure you can't have forgotten how dreadful he was that night he came here. I let him see how shocked I was. I know you were angry with me, and I thought it very unreasonable of you, because I did it on purpose, and it stopped him. You may say what you like, Liz, but it stopped him. Mrs. Havergill told Markham—yes, I know you don't think I ought to talk to Markham about David, but she began about it herself, and she is really interested, and thought I would like to know—well, she says David has never touched a drop since. Mrs. Havergill told her so. So you see, Liz, I haven't always been as bad for David as you seem to think. I don't know if you want him to go and marry Katie Ellerton, just out of pique. She's running after him worse than ever—I really do wonder she isn't ashamed, and if David's friends cast him off, well, she'll just snap him up, and then I should think you'd be sorry."

Elizabeth leaned her chin in her hand, and was silent for a moment. Then she said: "Molly, dear, why should we try and prevent David from going to see Katie Ellerton? He is in love with you, and it is very bad for him. If he saw less of you for a time it would give him a chance of getting over it. David is very unhappy just now. No one can fail to see that. He wants what you can't give him—rest, companionship, a home. If Katie cares for him, and can give him these things, let her give them. We have no business to stand in the way. Don't you see that?"

Elizabeth spoke sweetly and persuasively. She kept her eyes on her sister's face, and saw there, first, offence, and then interest—the birth of a new idea.

"Oh, well—if you don't mind," said Mary. "You are nearly as tiresome as Edward and Edward has been most dreadfully tiresome. I told him so. I said, 'Edward, I really never knew you could be so tiresome,' and it seemed to make him *worse*. I think, you know, that he is afraid that people will talk if David goes on coming here. Of course, that's absurd, I told him it was absurd. I said, 'Why, how on earth is any one to know that it isn't Elizabeth he comes to see?' And then, Edward became really violent. I didn't know he could be, but he was. He simply plunged up and down the room, and said: 'If he wants to see Elizabeth, then in Heaven's name let him see Elizabeth. Let him *marry* Elizabeth.' Oh, you mustn't mind, Liz," as Elizabeth's head went up, "it was only because he was so cross, and you and David are such old friends. There's nothing for you to *mind*."

She paused, stole a quick glance at Elizabeth, then looked away, and said in a tentative voice, "Liz, why don't you marry David?"

"Because he doesn't want me to, Molly," said Elizabeth. Her voice was very proud, and her head very high.

Mary half put out her hand, and drew it back again. She knew this mood of Elizabeth's, and it was one that silenced even her ready tongue. She was the little sister again for a moment, and Elizabeth the mother, sister, and ideal—all in one.

"Liz, I 'm sorry," she said in quite a small, humble voice.

When she had gone, Elizabeth sat on by the fire. She did not move for a long time. When she did move, it was to put up a hand to her face, which was wet with many hot, slow tears. Pride dies hard, and hurts to the very last.

CHAPTER XI

FORGOTTEN WAYS

I have forgotten all the ways of sleep,
  The endless, windless silence of my dream,
  The milk-white poppy meadows and the stream,
The dreaming water soft and still and deep—
  I have forgotten how that water flows,
  I have forgotten how the poppy grows,
I have forgotten all the ways of sleep.

IT was on an afternoon, a few days later, that David came into the hall of the Mottisfonts' house.

"Lord save us, he do look bad," was the thought in Markham's mind as she let him in. Aloud she said that she thought Mrs. Mottisfont was just going out. As she spoke, Mary came down the stairs, bringing with her a sweet scent of violets.

Mary was very obviously going out. She wore a white cloth dress, with dark furs, and there was a large bunch of mauve and white violets at her breast. She looked a little vexed when she saw David.

"Oh," she said, "I am just going out. I am so sorry, but I am afraid I must. Bazaars are tiresome things, but one must go to them, and I promised Mrs. Codrington that I would be there early. Elizabeth is in. She'll give you some tea. Markham, will you please tell Miss Elizabeth?

David came forward as she was speaking. There was a window above the front door, and as he came out of the shadow, and the light fell on his face, he saw Mary start a little. Her expression changed, and she said in a hesitating manner:

"Of course, Elizabeth may be busy, or she may be going out—I really don't know. Perhaps you had better come another day, David."

He read her clearly enough. She thought that he had been drinking, and hesitated to leave him with her sister. He had been about to say that he could not stop, but her suspicion raised a devil of obstinacy in him, and as Elizabeth came out of her room by way of the dining-room, he advanced to meet her, saying:

"Will you give me some tea, Elizabeth, or are you too busy?"

"Liz, come here," said Mary quickly. Her colour had risen at David's tone. She drew Elizabeth a little aside. "Liz, you'd better not," she whispered, "he looks so queer."

"Nonsense, Molly."

"I wish you wouldn't—"

"My dear Molly, are you going to begin to chaperone me?"

Mary tossed her head.

"Oh, if you don't *mind*," she said angrily, and went out, leaving Elizabeth with an odd sense of anticipation.

Elizabeth found David standing before the writing-table, and looking at himself in the little Dutch mirror which hung above it. He turned as she came in.

"Well," he said bitterly, "has Mary renounced the Bazaar in order to stay and protect you? I 'm not really as dangerous as she seems to think, though I am willing to admit that

I am not exactly ornamental. Give me some tea, and I'll not inflict myself on you for long."

Elizabeth smiled.

"You know very well that I like having you here," she said in her friendly voice. "Look at my flowers. Aren't they well forward? I really think that everything is a fortnight before its time this year. No, not that chair, David. This one is much more comfortable."

Markham was coming in with the tea as Elizabeth spoke. David sat silent. He watched the tiny flame of the spirit-lamp, the mingled flicker of firelight and daylight upon the silver, and the thin old china with its branching pattern of purple and yellow flowers. He drank as many cups of tea as Elizabeth gave him, and she talked a little in a desultory manner, until he had finished, and then sat in a silence that was not awkward, but companionable.

David made no effort to move, or speak. This was a pleasant room of Elizabeth's. The brown panels were warm in the firelight. They made a soft darkness that had nothing gloomy about it, and the room was full of flowers. The great brown crock full of daffodils stood on the window-ledge, and on the table which filled the angle between the window and the fireplace was another, in which stood a number of the tall yellow tulips which smell like Maréchal-Niel roses. Elizabeth's dress was brown, too. It was made of some soft stuff that made no sound when she moved. The room was very still, and very sweet, and the sweetness and the stillness were very grateful to David Blake. The thought came to him suddenly, that it was many years since he had sat like this in Elizabeth's room, and the silence had companioned them. Years ago he had been there often enough, and they had talked, read, argued, or been still, just as the spirit of the moment dictated. They had been good comrades, then, in the old days—the happy days of youth.

He looked across at Elizabeth and said suddenly:

"You are a very restful woman, Elizabeth."

She smiled at him without moving, and answered:

"I am glad if I rest you, David—I think you need rest."

"You sit so still. No one else sits so still."

Elizabeth laughed softly.

"That sounds as if I were a very inert sort of person," she said.

David frowned a little.

"No, it's not that. It is strength—force—stability. Only strong things keep still like that."

This was so like the old David, that it took Elizabeth back ten years at a leap. She was silent for a moment, gathering her courage. Then she said:

"David, you do need rest, and a change. Why don't you go away?"

She had thought he would be angry, but he was not angry. Instead, he answered her as the David of ten years ago might have done, with a misquotation.

"What is the good of a change? It's a case of—I myself am my own Heaven and Hell"; and his voice was the voice of a very weary man.

Elizabeth's eyes dwelt on him with a deep considering look.

"Yes, that's true," she said. "One has to find oneself. But it is easier to find oneself in clear country than in a fog. This place is not good for you, David. When I said you wanted a change, I didn't mean just for a time—I meant altogether. Why don't you go right away—leave it all behind you, and start again?"

He looked at her as if he might be angry, if he were not too tired.

"Because I won't run away," he said, with his voice back on the harsh note which had become habitual.

There was a pause. Elizabeth heard her own heart beat. The room was getting darker. A log fell in the fire.

Then David laughed bitterly.

"That sounded very fine, but it's just a flam. The truth is, not that I won't run away, but that I can't. I've not got the energy. I'm three parts broke, and it's all I can do to keep going at all. I couldn't start fresh, because I've got nothing to start with. If I could sleep for a week it would give me a chance, but I can't sleep. Skeffington has taken me in hand now, and out of three drugs he has given me, two made me feel as if I were going mad, and the third had no effect at all. I'm full of bromide now. It makes me sleepy, but it doesn't make me sleep. You don't know what it's like. My brain is drunk with sleep—marshy with it, water-logged—but there's always one point of consciousness left high and dry—tortured."

"Can't you sleep at all?"

"I suppose I do, or I should be mad in real earnest. Do I look mad, Elizabeth?"

She looked at him. His face was very white, except for a flushed patch high up on either cheek. His eyes were bloodshot and strained, but there was no madness in them.

"Is that what you are afraid of?"

"Yes, my God, yes," said David Blake, speaking only just above his breath.

"I don't think you need be afraid. I don't, really, David. You look very tired. You look as if you wanted sleep more than anything else in the world.,"

She spoke very gently. "Will you let me send you to sleep? I think I can."

"Does one ask a man who is dying of thirst if one may give him a drink?"

"Then I may?"

"If you can—but—" He broke off as Markham came in to clear away the tea. Elizabeth began to talk of trivialities. For a minute or two Markham came and went, but when she had taken away the tray, and the door was shut, there was silence again.

Elizabeth had turned her chair a little. She sat looking into the fire. She was not making pictures among the embers, as she sometimes did. Her eyes had a brooding look. Her honey-coloured hair looked like pale gold against the brown paneling behind her. She sat very still. David found it pleasant to watch her, pleasant to be here.

His whole head was stiff and numb with lack of sleep. Every muscle seemed stretched and every nerve taut. There was a dull, continuous pain at the back of his head. Thought seemed muffled, his faculties clogged. Two thirds of his brain was submerged, but in the remaining third consciousness flared like a flickering will-o'-the-wisp above a marsh.

David lay back in his chair. This was a peaceful place, a peaceful room. He had not meant to stay so long, but he had no desire to move. Slowly, slowly the tide of sleep mounted in him. Not, as often lately, with a sudden flooding wave which retreated again as suddenly, and left his brain reeling, but steadily, quietly, like the still rising of some peaceful, moon-drawn sea. He seemed to see that lifting tide. It was as deep and still as those still waters of which another David wrote. It rose and rose—the will-o'-the-wisp of consciousness ceased its tormented flickering, and he slept.

Elizabeth never turned her head. She heard his breathing deepen, until it was very slow and steady. There was no other sound except when an ember dropped. The light failed. Soon there was no light but the glow of the fire.

CHAPTER XII

THE GREY WOLF

I thought I saw the Grey Wolf's eyes
Look through the bars of night;
They drank the silver of the moon,
And the stars' pale chrysolite.
From star by star they took their toll,
And through the drained and darkened night
They sought my darkened soul.

DAVID slept for a couple of hours, and that night he slept more than he had done for weeks. Next night, however, there returned the old strain, the old yearning for oblivion, the old inability to compass it. In the week that followed David passed through a number of strange, mental phases. After that first sound sleep had relieved the tension of his brain, he told himself that he owed it to the delayed action of the bromide Skeffington had given him. But as the strain returned, though reason held him to this opinion still, out of the deep undercurrents of consciousness there rose before him a vision of Elizabeth, with the gift of sleep in her hand. He passed into a state of conflict, and out of this conflict there grew up a pride that would owe nothing to a woman, a resistance that called itself reason and independence. And then, as the desire for sleep dominated everything, conflict merged into a desire that Elizabeth should heal him, should make him sleep. And all through the week he did not think of Mary at all. The craving for her had been swallowed up by that other craving. Mary had raised this fever, but it had now reached a point at which he had become unconscious of her. It was Elizabeth who filled his thoughts. Not Elizabeth the woman, but Elizabeth the bearer of that gift of sleep. But this, too, was a phase, and had its reaction.

Towards the end of the week he finished his afternoon round by going to see an old Irish-woman, who had been in the hospital for an operation, and had since been dismissed as incurable. She was a plucky old soul, and a cheerful, but to-day David found her in a downcast mood.

"Sure, it's not the pain I'd be minding if I could get my sleep," she said. "Couldn't ye be after putting the least taste of something in my medicine, then, Doctor, dear?"

David had his finger on her pulse. He patted her hand kindly as he laid it down.

"Come, now, Mrs. Halloran," he said, "when I gave you that last bottle of medicine you said it made you sleep beautifully."

"Just for a bit it did," said Judy Halloran. "Sure, it was only for a bit, and now it's the devil's own nights I 'm having. Couldn't you be making it the least taste stronger, then?"

She looked at David rather piteously.

"Well, we must see," he said. "You finish that bottle, and then I'll see what I can do for you."

Mrs. Halloran closed her eyes for a minute. Then she opened them rather suddenly, shot a quick look at David, and said with an eager note in her voice:

"They do be saying that Miss Chantrey can make any one sleep. There was a friend of mine was after telling me about it. It was her daughter that had the sleep gone from her, and after Miss Chantrey came to see her, it was the fine nights she was having, and it's the strong woman she is now, entirely."

David got up rather abruptly.

"Come, now, Mrs. Halloran," he said, "you know as well as I do that that's all nonsense. But I daresay a visit from Miss Chantrey would cheer you up quite a lot. Would you like to see her? Shall I ask her to come in one day?"

"She'd be kindly welcome," said Judy Halloran.

David went home with the old conflict raging again. Skeffington had been urging him to see a specialist. He had always refused. But now, quite suddenly, he wired for an appointment.

He came down from town on a dark, rainy afternoon, feeling that he had built up a barrier between himself and superstition.

An hour later he was at the Mottisfonts' door, asking Markham if Mary was at home. Mary had gone out to tea, said Markham, and then volunteered, "Miss Elizabeth is in, sir."

David told himself that he had not intended to ask for Elizabeth. Why should he ask for Elizabeth? He could, however, hardly explain to Markham that it was not Elizabeth he wished to see, so he came in, and was somehow very glad to come.

Elizabeth had been reading aloud to herself. As he stood at the door he could hear the rise and fall of her voice. It was an old trick of hers. Ten years ago he had often stood on the threshold and listened, until rebuked by Elizabeth for eavesdropping.

He came in, and she said just in the old voice:

"You were listening, David."

But it was the David of to-day who responded wearily, "I beg your pardon, Elizabeth. Did you mind?"

"No, of course not. Sit down, David. What have you been doing with yourself?"

Instead of sitting down he walked to the window and looked out. The sky was one even grey, and, though the rain had ceased, heavy drops were falling from the roof and denting the earth in Elizabeth's window boxes, which were full of daffodils in bud. After a moment he turned and said impatiently, "How dark this room is!"

Elizabeth divined in him a reaction, a fear of what she had done, and might do. She knew very well why he had stayed away. Without replying she put out her hand and touched a switch on the wall. A tall lamp with a yellow shade sprang into view, and the whole room became filled with a soft, warm light.

David left the window, but still he did not sit. For a while he walked up and down restlessly, but at length came to a standstill between Elizabeth and the fire. He was so close to her that she had only to put out her hand and it would have touched his. He stood looking, now at the miniatures on the wall, now at the fire which burned with a steady red glow. He was half turned from Elizabeth, but she could see his face. It was strained and thin. The flesh had fallen away, leaving the great bones prominent.

It was Elizabeth who broke the silence, and she said what she had not meant to say.

"David, are you better? Are you sleeping?"

"No," he said shortly.

"And you won't let me help?"

"I didn't say so."

"Did you think I didn't know?" Elizabeth's voice was very sad.

They had fallen suddenly upon an intimate note. It was a note that he had never touched with Mary. That they should be talking like this filled him with a dazed surprise.

He as well as she was taking it for granted that she had given him sleep, and could give him sleep again.

He gave himself a sudden shake.

"I 'm going away," he said in a harder voice.

There was a pause.

"I 'm glad," said Elizabeth, and then there was silence again.

This time it was David who spoke, and he spoke in the hot, insistent tones of a man who argues a losing case.

"One can't go on not sleeping. That is what I said to old Wyatt Byng to-day."

"Sir Wyatt Byng?" said Elizabeth quickly.

"Yes—I saw him. Skeffington would have me see him, but what's the use? He swears I shall sleep, if I take the stuff he's given me—the latest French fad—but I don't sleep. I seem to have lost the way—and one can't go on."

He paused, and then said frowning:

"It's so odd—"

"Odd?"

"Yes—so odd—sleep. Such an odd thing. It was so easy once. Now it's so difficult that it can't be done. Why? No one knows. No one knows what sleep is—"

His voice trailed away. He was strung like a wire that is ready to snap, and on the borders of consciousness, just out of sight, something waited; he turned his head sharply, as if the thing he dreaded might be there—behind him—in the shadow.

Instead, he saw Elizabeth in a golden light like a halo. It swam before his tired eyes, a glow with a rainbow edge. Out of the heart of it she looked at him with serious, tender eyes.

Beyond, in the gloom, there lurked such a horror as made him catch his breath, and here at his side—in this room, peace, safety, and sleep—sleep, the one thing in heaven or earth desired and desirable.

A sort of shudder passed over him, and he repeated his own last words in a low, altered voice.

"One can't go on. Something must give way. Sometimes I feel as if it might give now—at any moment. Then there's madness—when one can't sleep. Am I going mad, Elizabeth?"

Elizabeth caught his hand and held it. He was so near that the impulse carried her away. Her clasp was strong, warm, and vital.

"No, my dear, no," she said.

Then with a catch in her voice:

"Oh, David—let me help you."

He shook his head in a slow, considering manner.

"No—there would be only one way—and that's not fair."

"What isn't fair, David?"

"You—to marry—me," he said, still in that slow, considering way. "You know, Elizabeth, I can't think very well. My head is all to pieces. But it's not fair, and I can't take your help—" He broke off frowning.

"David, it has nothing to do with that sort of thing," said Elizabeth very seriously. "It's only what I would do for any one."

She was shaken to the depths, but she kept her voice low and steady.

"Yes—it has—one can't take like that—"

"Because I 'm a woman? Just because I 'm a woman?"

Elizabeth looked up quickly and spoke quickly, because she knew that if she stopped to think she would not speak at all.

"And if we were married?"

"Then it would be different," said David Blake.

His voice was not like his usual voice. It sounded like the voice of a man who was puzzled, who was trying to recall something of which he has seen glimpses. Was it something from the past, or something from the future?

Elizabeth got up and stood as he was standing—one hand on the oak shelf above the fireplace—the other clenched at her side.

"David, are you asking me to marry you?" she said.

He raised his head, half startled. The silence that followed her question seemed to fill the room and shake it. His will shook too, drawn this way and that by forces that were above and beyond them both.

Elizabeth did not look at him. She did not know what he would answer, and all their lives hung on that answer of his. She held her breath, and it seemed to her that she was holding her will too. She was suddenly, overpoweringly conscious of her own strength, her own vital force and power. If she let this force go out to David now—in his weakness! It was the greatest temptation that she had ever known, and, after one shuddering moment, she turned from it in horror. She kept her will, her strength, her vital powers in a strong grip. No influence of hers must touch or sway him now. Her heart stopped beating. Her very life seemed to be suspended. Then she heard David say:

"Would you marry me, Elizabeth?" His tone was a wondering one. It broke the tension. She turned her head a little and said:

"Yes—if you needed me."

"Need—need—I think I should sleep—and if I don't sleep I shall go mad. But, perhaps I shall go mad anyhow. You must not marry me if I am going mad."

"You won't go mad."

"You think not? There is something that shakes all the time. It never stops. It goes on always. I think that is why I don't sleep. But when I am with you it seems to stop. I don't know why, but it does seem to stop, just whilst I am with you."

"It will stop altogether when you get your sleep back."

"Oh, yes."

The half-dreamy note went out of his voice, and the note of intimate self-revealing. Elizabeth noticed the change at once.

"When do you go away, and where do you go?" she asked.

"Switzerland, I think. I could get away by the 3rd of April."

David was trying to think, but his head was very tired. He must go away. He must have a change. They all said that. But it was no use for him to go away if he did not sleep. He must have sleep. But if Elizabeth were with him he would sleep. Elizabeth must come with him. If they were married at once she could come with him, and then he would sleep. But it was so soon. He spoke his thought aloud.

"You wouldn't marry me first, I suppose? You wouldn't come with me?"

"Why not?" said Elizabeth quietly. The quietness hid the greatest effort of her life. "If you want me, I will come. I only want to help you, and if I can help you best that way—"

David let himself sink into a chair, and began to talk a little of plans, wearily and with an effort. He had to force his brain to make it work at all. All these details, these plans, these conventions seemed to him irrelevant and burdensome.

He got up to go as the clock struck seven.

Elizabeth put out her hand to him as she had always done.

"And you will let me help you?"

"No, not yet—not till afterwards," he said.

"It makes no difference, David, you know. It is just what I would do for any one who wanted it—"

He shook his head. There was a reaction upon him, a withdrawal.

"Not yet—not till afterwards. I'll give old Byng's stuff a chance," he said obstinately, and then went out with just a bare good-night.

CHAPTER XIII

MARCH GOES OUT

I thought I saw the Grey Wolf's eyes.
　　The sun was gone away,
Most unendurably gone down,
　　With all delights of day.
I cried aloud for light, and all
The light was dead and done away,
　　And no one answered to my call.

EDWARD was, perhaps, the person best pleased at the news of Elizabeth's engagement. He had been, as Mary phrased it, "very much put out." Put out, in fact, to the point of wondering whether he could possibly nerve himself to tell David that he came too often to the house. He had an affection for David, and he was under an obligation to him, but there were limits—during the last fortnight he had very frequently explained to Mary that there were limits. Whether he would ever have got as far as explaining this to David remains amongst the lesser mysteries of life. Mary did not take the explanation in what Edward considered at all a proper spirit. She bridled, looked very pretty, talked about good influences, and was much offended when Edward lost his temper. He lost it to the extent of consigning good influences to a place with which they are not usually connected, though the way to it is said to be paved with good intentions. Mary had a temper, too. It took her out of the room with a bang of the door, but she subsequently cried herself sick because Edward had sworn at her.

There was a reconciliation, but Edward was not as penitent as Mary thought he should have been. David became a sore point with both of them, and Edward, at least, was unfeignedly pleased at what he considered a happy solution of the difficulty. He was fond of Elizabeth, but it would certainly be more agreeable to have the whole house at his own disposal. He had always thought that Elizabeth's little brown room would be the very place for his collections. He fell to estimating the probable cost of lining the whole wall-space with cabinets.

Mary was not quite as pleased as Edward.

"You know, Liz," she said, "I am very *glad* that David should marry. I think he wants a home. But I don't think you ought to marry him until he's *better*. He looks dreadful. And a fortnight's engagement—I can't *think* what people will say—one ought to consider that."

"Oh, Molly, you are too young for the part of Mrs. Grundy," said Elizabeth, laughing.

Mary coloured and said:

"It's all very well, Liz, but people will talk."

"Well, Molly, and if they do? What is there for them to say? It is all very simple, really. No one can help seeing how ill David is, and I think every one would understand my wanting to be with him. People are really quite human and understanding if they are taken the right way."

"But a fortnight," said Mary, frowning. "Why, Liz, you will not be able to get your things!" And she was shocked beyond words when Elizabeth betrayed a complete indifference as to whether she had any new things at all.

The wedding was fixed for the 3rd of April, and the days passed. David made the necessary arrangements with a growing sense of detachment. The matter was out of his hands.

For a week the new drug gave him sleep, a sleep full of brilliant dreams, strange flashes of light, and bursts of unbearable colour. He woke from it with a blinding headache and a sense of strain beyond that induced by insomnia. Towards the end of the week he stopped taking the drug. The headache had become unendurable. This state was worse than the last.

On the last day of March he came to Elizabeth and told her that their marriage must be deferred.

"Ronnie Ellerton is very ill," he said; "I can't go away."

"But David, you *must*—"

He shook his head. The obstinacy of illness was upon him.

"I can't—and I won't," he declared. Then, as if realizing that he owed her some explanation, he added:

"He's so spoilt. Why are women such fools? He's never been made to do anything he didn't like. He won't take food or medicine, and I 'm the only person who has the least authority over him. And she's half crazy with anxiety, poor soul. I have promised not to go until he's round the corner. It's only a matter of a day or two, so we must just put it off."

Elizabeth put her hand on his arm.

"David, we need not put off the marriage," she said in her most ordinary tones. "You see, if we are married, we could start off as soon as the child was better."

She had it in her mind that unless David would let her help him soon, he would be past helping.

He looked at her indifferently. "You will stay here?"

"Not unless you wish," she answered.

"I? Oh! it is for you to say."

There was no interest in his tone. If he thought of anything it was of Ronnie Ellerton. A complete apathy had descended upon him. Nothing was real, nothing mattered. Health—sanity—rest—these were only names. They meant nothing. Only when he turned to his work, his brain still moved with the precision of a machine, regularly, correctly.

He did not tell her either then or ever, that Katie Ellerton had broken down and spoken bitter words about his marriage.

"I've nothing but Ronnie—nothing but Ronnie—and you will go away with her and he will die. I know he will die if you go. Can't she spare you just for two days—or three—to save Ronnie's life? Promise me you won't go till he is safe—promise—promise."

And David had promised, taking in what she had said about the child, but only half grasping the import of her frantic appeal. Neither he nor she were real people to him just now. Only Ronnie was real—Ronnie, who was ill, and his patient.

Elizabeth went through the next two days with a heavy heart. She had to meet Mary's questions, her objections, her disapprobations, and it was all just a little more than she could bear.

On the night before the wedding, Mary left Edward upstairs and came to sit beside Elizabeth's fire. Elizabeth would rather have been alone, and yet she was pleased that Mary cared to come. If only she would let all vexed questions be—it seemed as if she would, for her mood was a silent one. She sat for a long time without speaking, then, with an impulsive movement, she slid out of her chair and knelt at Elizabeth's side.

"Oh, Liz, I've been cross. I know I have. I know you've thought me cross. But it's because I've been unhappy—Liz, I 'm not *happy* about you—"

Elizabeth put her hand on Mary's shoulder for a moment.

"Don't be unhappy, Molly," she said, in rather an unsteady voice.

"But I am, Liz, I am—I can't help it—I have talked, and worried you, and have been cross, but all the time I've been most dreadfully unhappy. Oh, Liz, don't do it—don't!"

"Molly, dear—"

"No, I know it's no use—you won't listen—" and Mary drew away and dabbed her eyes with a fragmentary apology for a pocket-handkerchief.

"Molly, please—"

Mary nodded.

"Yes, Liz, I know. I won't—I didn't mean to—"

There was a little silence. Then with a sudden choking sob, Mary turned and said:

"I can't *bear* it. Oh, Liz, you ought to be loved so much. You ought to marry some one who loves you—*really*—. And I don't think David does. Liz, does he love you—does he?"

The sound of her own words frightened her a little, but Elizabeth answered very gently and sadly:

"No, Molly, but he needs me."

Mary was silenced. Here was something beyond her. She put her arms round Elizabeth and held her very tightly for a moment. Then she released her with a sob, and ran crying from the room.

CHAPTER XIV

THE GOLDEN WIND

Then far, oh, very far away,
   The Wind began to rise,
The Sun, the Moon, the Stars were gone,
   I saw the Grey Wolf's eyes.
The Wind rose up and rising, shone,
   I saw it shine, I saw it rise,
And suddenly the dark was gone.

DAVID BLAKE was married to Elizabeth Chantrey at half-past two of an April day. Edward and Mary Mottisfont were the only witnesses, with the exception of the verger, who considered himself a most important person on these occasions, when he invariably appeared to be more priestly than the rector and more indispensable than the bridegroom.

It requires no practice to be a bridegroom but years, if not generations, go to the making of the perfect verger. This verger was the son and the grandson of vergers. He was the perfect verger. He stood during the service and disapproved of David's grey pallor, his shaking hand, and his unsteady voice. His black gown imparted a funerary air to the proceedings.

"Drinking, that's what he'd been," he told his wife, and his wife said, "Oh, William," as one who makes response to an officiating priest.

But he wronged David, who was not drunk—only starved for lack of sleep, and strung to the breaking point. His voice stumbled over the words in which he took Elizabeth to be his wedded wife and trailed away to a whisper at the conclusion.

A gusty wind beat against the long grey windows, and between the gusts the heavy rain thudded on the roof above.

Mary shivered in the vestry as she kissed Elizabeth and wished her joy. Then she turned to David and kissed him too. He was her brother now, and there would be no more nonsense. Edward frowned, David stiffened, and Elizabeth, standing near him, was aware that all his muscles had become rigid.

Elizabeth and David went out by the vestry door, and stood a moment on the step. The rain had ceased quite suddenly in the April fashion. The sky was very black overhead and the air was full of a wet wind, but far down to the right the water meadows lay bathed in a clear sweet sunshine, and the west was as blue as a turquoise. Between the blue of the sky and the bright emerald of the grass, the horizon showed faintly golden, and a broken patch of rainbow light glowed against the nearest dark cloud.

David and Elizabeth walked to their home in silence. Mrs. Havergill awaited them with an air of mournful importance. She had prepared coffee and a cake with much almond icing and the word "Welcome" inscribed upon it in silver comfits. Elizabeth ate a piece of cake from a sense of duty, and David drank cup after cup of black coffee, and then sat in a sort of stupor of fatigue until roused by the sound of the telephone bell.

After a minute or two he came back into the room.

"Ronnie is worse," he said shortly. There was a change in him. He had pulled himself together. His voice was stronger.

"He's worse. I must go at once. Don't wait dinner, and don't sit up. I may have to stay all night."

When he had gone, Elizabeth went upstairs to unpack. Mrs. Havergill followed her.

"You 'avn't been in this room since Mrs. Blake was took."

"It's a very nice room," said Elizabeth.

"All this furniture," said Mrs. Havergill, "come out of the 'ouse in the 'Igh Street. That old mahogany press, Mrs. Blake set a lot of store by, and the bed, too. Ah! pore thing, I suppose she little thought as 'ow she'd come to die in it."

The bed was a fine old four-poster, with a carved foot-rail. Elizabeth went past it to the windows, of which there were three, set casement fashion, at the end of the room, with a wide low window-seat running beneath them.

She got rid of Mrs. Havergill without hurting her feelings. Then she knelt on the seat, and looked out. She saw the river beneath her, and a line of trees in the first green mist of their new leaves. The river was dark and bright in patches, and the wind sang above it. Elizabeth's heart was glad of this place. It was a thing she loved—to see green trees and bright water, and to hear the wind go by above the stream.

When she had unpacked and put everything away, she stood for a moment, and then opened the door that led through into David's room. It was getting dark in here, for the room faced the east. Elizabeth went to the window and looked out. The sky was full of clouds, and the promise of rain.

It was very late before David came home. At ten, Elizabeth sent the servants to bed. There was cold supper laid in the dining-room, and soup in a covered pan by the side of the fire. Elizabeth sat by the lamp and sewed. Every now and then she lifted her head and listened. Then she sewed again.

At twelve o'clock David put his key into the latch, and the door opened with a little click and then shut again.

David was a long time coming in. He came in slowly, and sat down upon the first chair he touched.

"He'll do," he said in an exhausted voice.

"I 'm so glad," said Elizabeth.

She knelt by the fire, and poured some of the soup into a cup. Then she held it out to him, and he drank, taking long draughts. After that she put food before him, and he ate in a dazed, mechanical fashion.

When he had finished, he sat staring at Elizabeth, with his elbows on the table, and his head between his hands.

"Ronnie is asleep—he'll do." And then with sudden passion: "My God, if I could sleep!"

"You will, David," said Elizabeth. She put her hand on his arm, and he turned his head a little, still staring at her.

"No, I don't sleep," he said. "Everything else sleeps—*Die Vöglein ruhen im Walde.* How does it go?"

"*Warte nur, balde ruhest du auch,*" said Elizabeth in her tranquil voice.

"No," said David, "I can't get in. It was so easy once—but now I can't get in. The silent city of sleep has long, smooth walls—I can't find the gate; I grope along the wall all night, hour after hour. A hundred times I think I have found the door. Sometimes there is a flashing sword that bars the way, sometimes the wall closes—closes as I pass the threshold. There's no way in. The walls are smooth—all smooth—you can't get in."

He spoke, not wildly, but in a low, muttering way. Elizabeth touched his hand. It was very hot.

"Come, David," she said, "it is late." She drew him to his feet, and he walked uncertainly, and leaned on her shoulder as they went up the stair. Once in his room, he sank again upon a chair. He let her help him, but when she knelt, and would have unlaced his boots, he roused himself.

"No, you are not to," he said with a sudden anger in his voice, and he took them off, and then let her help him again.

When he was in bed, Elizabeth stood by him for a moment.

"Are you comfortable?" she asked.

"If I could sleep," he said, only just above his breath. "If I could."

"Oh, but you will," said Elizabeth. "Don't be afraid, David. It's all right."

She set the door into her room ajar and then sat down by the window, and looked out at the night. The blind was up. The night was dark and clear. There were stars, many little glittering points. It was very still. Elizabeth fixed her eyes upon the sky, but after a minute or two she did not see it at all. Her mind was full of David and his need. This tortured, sleepless state of his had no reality. How could it compass and oppress the immortal image of God? Her thought rose into peace. Elizabeth opened her mind to the Divine light. Her will rested. She was conscious only of that radiant peace. It enwrapped her, it enwrapped David. In it they lived and moved and had their being. In it they were real and vital creatures. To lapse from consciousness of it, was to fall upon a formless, baseless dream, wherein were the shadows of evil. These shadows had no reality. Brought to the light, they faded, leaving only that peace—that radiance. Elizabeth's eyes were opened. She saw the Wings of Peace.

And David slept.

CHAPTER XV

LOVE MUST TO SCHOOL

Love must to school to learn his alphabet,
His wings are shorn, his eyes are dim and wet.
He pores on books that once he knew by heart—
Poor, foolish Love, to wander and forget.

ELIZABETH sat quite motionless for half an hour. Then she stirred, bent her head for a moment, whilst she listened to David's regular breathing, and then rose to her feet. She passed through the open door into her own room, and undressed in the dark. Then she lay down and slept.

Three times during the night she woke and listened. But David still slept. When she woke up for the third time, the room was full of the greyness of the dawn. She got up and closed the door between the two rooms.

Then she lay waking. It had been a strange wedding night.

The day dawned cloudy, but broke at noon into a cloudless warmth that was more like June than April.

"Take me down the river," said Elizabeth, and they rowed down for half a mile, and turned the boat into a water-lane where budding willows swept down on either side, and brushed the stream.

David was very well content to lie in the sun. The strain was gone from him, leaving behind it a weariness beyond words. Every limb, every muscle, every nerve was relaxed. There was a great peace upon him. The air tasted sweet. The light was a pleasant thing. The sky was blue, and so was Elizabeth's dress, and Elizabeth was a very reposeful person. She did not fidget and she did not chatter. When she spoke it was of pleasant things.

David recalled a day, ten years ago, when he had sat with her in this very place. He could see himself, full of enthusiasm, full of youth. He could remember how he had talked, and how Elizabeth had listened. She was just the same now. It was he who had changed. Ten years ago seemed to him a very pleasant time, a very pleasant memory. Pictures rose before him—stray words—stray recollections running into a long, soft blur.

They came home in the dusk.

"Are you going to see Ronnie again?" said Elizabeth, as they landed.

"Yes; he couldn't be doing better, but I'll look in, and to-morrow Skeffington will go with me so as to get him broken in to the change. We ought to get away all right now."

David waked next day to find the sun shining in at his uncurtained window. From where he lay he could see the young blue of the sky, and all the room seemed full of the sun's gold. David lay in a lazy contentment watching the motes that danced in a long shining beam. There was a new stir of life in his veins. He stretched out his limbs and was glad of their strength. The sweetness and the glory and the promise of the spring slid into his blood and fired it.

"Mary," he said, still between sleeping and waking—and with the name, memory woke. Suddenly his brain was very clear. He looked straight ahead and saw the door that led into the other room—the room that had been his mother's. Elizabeth was in that room.

He had married Elizabeth—she was his wife. He lay quite still and stared at the door. Elizabeth Chantrey was Elizabeth Blake. She was his wife—and Mary—

A sudden spasm of laughter caught David by the throat. Mary was what she had promised to be—his sister; Mary was his sister. The spasm of laughter passed, and with it the stir in David's blood. He was quite cool now. He lay staring at that closed door, and faced the situation.

It was a damnable situation, he decided. He felt as a man might feel who wakes from the delirium of weeks, to find that in his madness he has done some intolerable, some irrevocable thing. A man who does not sleep is a man who is not wholly sane. David looked back and followed the events of the last few months with a critical detachment.

He saw the strain growing and growing until, in the end, on the brink of the abyss, he had snatched at the relief which Elizabeth offered, as a man who dies of thirst will snatch at water. Well—he had taken Elizabeth's draught of water, his thirst was quenched, he was his own man again. No, never his own man any more. Never free any more— Elizabeth's debtor—Elizabeth's husband.

David set his face like a flint—he would pay his debt.

He went out as soon as he had breakfasted and walked for a couple of hours. It was a little after noon when he came into the drawing-room where Elizabeth was.

The floor was covered with a great many yards of green stuff which she was cutting into curtain lengths. As David came in, she looked up and smiled.

"Oh, please," she said, "if you wouldn't mind, I shall cut them so much better if you hold one end."

David knelt down and held the stuff, whilst Elizabeth cut it. She came quite close to him at the end, smiled again, and took away the two pieces which he still clutched helplessly.

"That's beautiful," she said, and sat down and began to sew.

David watched her in silence. If she found his gaze embarrassing, she showed no sign.

"We can start to-morrow," he said at last. He gave a list of trains, stopping-places, and hotels, paused at the end of it, walked to the window, and then, turning, said with an effort:

"This has been a bad beginning for you, my dear—you've been very good to me. You deserve a better bargain, but I'll do my best."

Elizabeth did not speak at once. David thought that she was not going to speak at all, but after what seemed like a long time she said:

"David!" and then stopped.

There was a good deal of colour in her cheeks. David saw that she, too, was making an effort

"Well," he said, and his voice was more natural.

"David," said Elizabeth, "what did you mean by 'doing your best'?"

David met her eyes. He had always liked Elizabeth's eyes. They were so very clear.

"I meant that I'd do my best to make you a good husband," he said quite simply.

Elizabeth's colour rose higher still. She continued to look at David, because she would have considered it cowardly to look away.

"A good husband to my good wife," she said. "But, David, I don't think you want a wife just now."

David came across the room and sat down by the table at which Elizabeth was working.

"Then why did you marry me, Elizabeth?" he asked.

Elizabeth did not turn her head at once.

"I think what we both want just now," she said, "is friendship." Her voice was low, but she kept it steady. "The sort of friendship that is one side of marriage. It is not really possible for a man and a woman to be friends in that sort of way unless they are married. I think you want a friend—I know I do. I think you have been very lonely—one is lonely, and it is worse for a man. He can't get the home-feeling, and he misses it. You did not marry me because you needed a wife. I don't think you do. When you want a wife, I will be your wife, but just now—"

She broke off. She did not look at David, but David looked at her. He saw how tightly her hands were clasped, he saw the colour flushing in her cheeks. She had great self-control, but that she was deeply moved was very evident.

All at once, he became conscious of great fatigue. He had walked far and in considerable distress of mind. He had put a very strong constraint upon himself. He rested his head on his hand and tried to think. Elizabeth did not speak again. After a time he raised his head. Elizabeth was watching him—her eyes were very soft. A sense of relief came upon David. Just to drift—just to let things go on in the old way, on the old lines. Not for always—just for a time—until he had put Mary out of his thought. Their marriage was not an ordinary one. It was for Elizabeth to make what terms she would. And it was a relief—yes, no doubt it was a relief.

"If I say, Yes," he said, "it is only for a time. It is not a very possible situation, you know, Elizabeth—not possible at all in most cases. But just now, just for the present, I admit your right to choose."

Elizabeth's hands relaxed.

"Thank you, David," she said.

CHAPTER XVI

FRIENDSHIP

See, God is everywhere,
Where, then, is care?
There is no night in Him,
Then how can we grow dim?
There is no room for pain or fear
Since God is Love, and Love is here.

The full cup lowered down into the sea,
Is full continually,
How can it lose one drop when all around
The endless floods abound?
So we in Him no part of Life can lose,
For all is ours to use.

DAVID found himself enjoying his holiday a good deal. Blue skies and shining air, clear cold of the snows and radiant warmth of the spring sun, sweet sleep by night and pleasant companionship by day—all these were his portion. His own content surprised him. He had been so long in the dark places that he could scarcely believe that the shadow was gone, and the day clear again. He had been prepared to struggle manfully against the feeling for Mary which had haunted and tormented him for so long. To his surprise, he found that this feeling fell into line with the other symptoms of his illness. He shrank from thinking of it, as he shrank from thinking of his craving for drink, his sleepless nights, and his dread of madness. It was all a part of the same bad dream—a shadow among shadows, in a world of gloom from which he had escaped.

Elizabeth was a very good companion. It was too early to climb, but they took long walks, shared picnic meals, and talked or were silent just as the spirit moved them. It was the old boy and girl companionship come back, and it was a very restful thing. One day, when they had been married about a fortnight, David said suddenly:

"How did you do it, Elizabeth?"

They were sitting on a grassy slope, looking over a wide valley where blue mists lay. A little wind was blowing, and the upper air was clear. The grass on which they sat was short. It was full of innumerable small white and purple anemones. Elizabeth was sitting on the grass, watching the flowers, and touching first one and then another with the tips of her fingers.

"All these little white ones have a violet stain at the back of each petal," was the last thing that she had said, but when David spoke she looked up, a little startled.

He was lying full length on a narrow ledge just above her, with his cap over his eyes to shield them from the sun, which was very bright.

"How did you do it, Elizabeth?" said David Blake.

Elizabeth hesitated. She could not see his face.

"What do you mean?"

"How did you do it? Was it hypnotism?"

"Oh, no—" There was real horror in her voice.

"It must have been."

She was silent for a moment. Then she said:

"Do you remember how interested we used to be in hypnotism, David?"

"Yes, that's partly what made me think of it."

"We read everything we could lay hands on—all the books on psychic phenomena—Charcot's experiments—everything. And do you remember the conclusion we came to?"

"What was it?"

"I don't think you've forgotten. I can remember you stamping up and down my little room and saying, 'It's a *damnable* thing, Elizabeth, a perfectly damnable thing. There's *no* end, absolutely none to the extent to which it undermines everything—I believe it is a much more real devil than any that the theologies produce.' That's what you said nine years ago, David, and I agreed with you. We used quite a lot of strong language between us, and I don't feel called upon to retract any of it. Hypnotism is a damnable thing."

David pushed the cap back from his eyes as Elizabeth spoke, and raised himself on his elbow, so that he could see her face.

"There are degrees," he said, "and it's very hard to define. How would you define it?"

"It's not easy. 'The unlawful influence of one mind over another'?"

"That's begging the question. At what point does it become unlawful?—that's the crux."

"I suppose at the point when force of will overbears sense—reason—conscience. You may persuade a man to lend you money, but you mayn't pick his pocket or hypnotise him."

David laughed.

"How practical!"

Then very suddenly:

"So it wasn't hypnotism. Are you *sure*?"

"Yes, quite sure."

"But can you be sure? There's such a thing as the unconscious exercise of will power."

Elizabeth shook her head.

"There is nothing in the least unconscious in what I do. I know very well what I am about, and I know enough about hypnotism to know that it is not that. I don't use my will at all."

"What do you do? How is it done?" His tone was interested.

"I think," said Elizabeth slowly, "that it is done by *realizing*, by getting into touch with Reality. Things like sleeplessness, pain, and strain aren't right—they aren't normal. They are like bad dreams. If one wakes—if one sees the reality—the dream is gone."

She spoke as if she were struggling to find words for some idea which filled her mind, but was hard to put into a communicable shape.

"It is life on the Fourth Dimension," she said at last.

"Yes," said David, "go on." There was a slightly quizzical look in his eyes, but he was interested. "What do you mean by the Fourth Dimension?"

"We used to talk of that too, and lately I have thought about it a lot."

"Yes?"

"It is so hard to put into words. Fourth Dimensional things won't get into Third Dimensional words. One has to try and try, and then a little scrap of the meaning comes through. That is why there are so many creeds, so many sects. They are all an attempt to express—and one can't really express the thing. I can't say it, I can only feel it. It is limitless, and words are limited. There are no bounds or barriers. Take Thought, for instance—that is Fourth Dimensional—and Love. Religion is a purely Fourth Dimensional thing, and we all guess and translate as best we may. In all religions that have life, apprehension rises above the creed and reaches out to the Real—the untranslatable."

"Yes, that's true; but go on—define the Fourth Dimension."

"I can see it, you know. It's another plane. It is the plane which permeates and inter-penetrates all other planes—universal, eternal, unchanging. It's like the Fire of God—searching all things. It is the plane of Reality. Nothing is real which is not universal and unchanging and eternal. If one can realize that plane, one is amongst the realities, and all that is unreal goes out. 'There is no life but the Life of God, no consciousness but the Divine Consciousness.' I think that is the best definition of all: 'the Divine Consciousness.'"

He did not know that she was quoting, and he did not answer her or speak at all for some time. But at last he said:

"So I slept, because you saw me in the Divine Consciousness; is that it?"

"Something like that."

"You didn't will that I should sleep?"

"Oh, no."

"Are you doing it still?"

"Yes."

"Every night?"

"Yes," said Elizabeth again.

David sat up. The mists in the valley beneath were golden, for the sun had dropped. As he looked, the gold turned grey, and the shadow of darkness to come rose out of the valley's depths, though the hill-slope on which they sat was warm and sunny yet. David turned and saw that Elizabeth was watching him.

"I want you to stop whatever it is you do," he said abruptly.

"Very well."

"I 'm not as ungrateful as that sounds—" He broke off, and Elizabeth said quickly:

"Oh, no."

"You don't think it?"

"Why should I? You are well again. You don't need my help any more."

A shadow like the shadow of evening came over her as she spoke, but her smile betrayed nothing.

They walked back to the hotel in silence.

David had wondered if he would sleep. He slept all night, the sweet sound sleep of health and a mind unburdened.

It was Elizabeth who did not sleep. She had walked with him through the valley of the shadow and he had come out of it a whole man again. Was she to cling to the shadow, because in the shadow David had clung to her? It came to that. She drove the thought home, and did not shirk the pain of it. They were come out into the light, and in the light he had no need of her. But this was not full daylight in which they walked—it was only the first chill grey of the dawn, and there is always a need of Love. Love needs must give, and giving, blesses and is blessed, for Love is of the realities—a thing immutable and all-pervading. No man can shut out Love.

CHAPTER XVII

THE DREAM

My hand has never touched your hand, I have not seen your face,
    No sound of any spoken word has passed between us two—
Yet night by night I come to you in some unearthly place,
    And all my dreams of day and night are dreams of love and you.

The moon has never shone on us together in our sleep,
    The sun has never seen us kiss beneath the arch of day,
Your eyes have never looked in mine—your soul has looked so deep,
    That all the sundering veils of sense are drawn and done away.

My lids are sealed with more than sleep, but I am lapped in light,
    Your soul draws near, and yet more near, till both our souls are one.
In that strange place of our content is neither day nor night,
    No end and no beginning, whilst the timeless aeons run.

DAVID came home after his month's holiday as hard and healthy as a man may be. Elizabeth was well content. She and David were friends. He liked her company, he ate and slept, he was well, and he laughed sometimes as the old David had laughed.

"Don't you think your master looks well, Mrs. Havergill?" she said quite gaily.

Mrs. Havergill sighed.

"He do look well," she admitted; "but there, ma'am, there's no saying—it isn't looks as we can go by. In my own family now, there was my sister Sarah. She was a fine, fresh-looking woman. Old Dr. Jones he met her out walking, as it might be on the Thursday.

"'Well, Miss Sarah, you *do* look well,' he says—and there, 't weren't but the following Tuesday as she was took. 'Who'd ha' thought it,' he says. 'In the midst of life we are in death,' and that's a true word. And my brother 'Enry now, 'e never look so well in all 'is life as when he was laying in 'is coffin."

Elizabeth could afford to laugh.

"Oh, Mrs. Havergill, do be cheerful," she implored; "it would be so much better for you."

Mrs. Havergill looked injured.

"I don't see as we 're sent into this world to be cheerful," she said, with the air of one who reproves unchristian levity.

"Oh, but we are—we really are," said Elizabeth.

Mrs. Havergill shook her head.

"Let them be cheerful as has no troubles," she remarked. "I've 'ad mine, and a-plenty," and she went out of the room, sighing.

Mary ran in to see her sister quite early on the morning after their return.

"Well, Liz—no, let me *look* at you—I'll kiss you in a minute. Are you *happy*—you wrote dreadful guide-book letters, that I tore up and put in the fire."

"Oh, Molly."

"Yes, they were—exactly like Baedeker, only worse. All about mountains and flowers and the nice air, and 'David is quite well again.' As if *anyone* wanted to hear about mountains and flowers from a person on her honeymoon. Are you *happy*, Liz?"

"Don't I look happy?" said Elizabeth laughing.

"Yes, you do." Mary looked at her considering. "You *do*. Is it all right, Liz, *really* all right?"

"Yes, it's really all right, Molly," said Elizabeth, and then she began to talk of other things.

Mary kissed her very affectionately when she went away, but at the door she turned, frowning.

"I expect you wrote *reams* to Agneta," she said, and then shut the door quickly before Elizabeth had time to answer.

David was out when Mary came, and it so happened that for two or three days they did not meet. He had come to dread the meeting. His passion for Mary was dead. He was afraid lest her presence, her voice, should raise the dead and bring it forth again in its garment of glamour and pain. Then on Sunday he came in to find Mary sitting there with Elizabeth in the twilight. She jumped up as he came in, and held out her hand.

"Well, David, you are a nice brother—never to have come and seen me. Busy? Yes, of course you've been busy, but you might have squeezed in a visit to me, amongst all the visits to sick old ladies and naughty little boys. Oh, *do* you know, Katie Ellerton has gone away? She took Ronnie to Brighton for a change, and then wrote and said she wasn't coming back. I believe she is going to live with a brother who is a solicitor down there. And she's selling her furniture, so if you *want* extra things you might get them cheap."

"That's Elizabeth's department," said David, laughing.

"Well, this is for you both. When will you come to dinner? On Tuesday? Yes, do. Talk about being busy. Edward's busy, if you like. I never see him, and he's quite worried. Liz, you remember Jack Webster? Well, you know he's on the West Coast, and he's sent Edward a whole case of things—frightfully exciting specimens, two centipedes he's wanted for ever so long, and a spider that Jack says is new. And Edward has never even had time to open the case. That shows you! It's accounts, I believe. Edward does hate accounts."

When she had gone David sat silent for a long time. It was the old Mary, and prettier than ever. He had never seen her looking prettier, but his feeling for her was gone. He could look at her quite dispassionately, and wonder over the old unreasoning thrill. And what a chatterbox she was. Thank Heaven, she had had the sense to marry Edward, who was really not such a bad sort. Poor Edward. He laughed aloud suddenly, and Elizabeth looked up asked:

"What is it?"

"Edward and the case he can't open, and the centipedes he can't play with," he said, still laughing. "Poor old Edward! What it is to have a conscience. I wonder he doesn't have a midnight orgy with the centipedes, but I suppose Mary sees to that."

It was that night that David dreamed his dream again. All these months it had never come to him. Amongst the many dreams that had haunted his sick brain, there had been no hint of this one. He had wondered about it sometimes. And now it returned. In the first deep sleep that comes to a healthy man he dreamed it.

He heard the wind blowing—that was the beginning of it. It came from the far distances of space, and it passed on again to the far distances beyond. David heard it blow, but his eyes were darkened. Then suddenly he saw. His feet were on the shining sand, the sand that shone because a golden moon looked down upon it from a clear sky, and the tide had left it wet.

David stood upon the shining sand, and saw the Woman of the Dream stand where the moon track ceased at the sea's rim. The moon was behind her head, and the wind blew out her hair. He stood as he had stood a hundred times, and as he had longed a hundred times to see the Woman's face, so he longed now. He moved to go to her, and the wind blew about him in his dream.

Elizabeth had sat late in her room. There was a book in her hand, but after a time she did not read. The night was very warm. She got up and opened the window wide. The moon was low and nearly full, and a wind blew out of the west—such a warm wind, full of the scent of green, growing things. Elizabeth put out the light and stood by the window, drawing long breaths. It seemed as if the wind were blowing right through her. It beat upon her uncovered throat, and the touch of it was like something alive. It sang in her ears, and Elizabeth's blood sang too.

And then, quite suddenly, she heard a sound that stopped her heart. She heard the handle of the door between her room and David's turn softly, and she heard a step upon the threshold. All her life was at her heart, waiting. She could neither move, nor speak, nor draw her breath. And the wind blew out her long white dress, and the wind blew out her hair. As in a trance between one world and the next, she heard a voice in the room. It was David's voice, and yet not David's voice, and it shook the very foundations of her being.

"Turn round and let me see your face, Woman of my Dream," said David Blake.

Elizabeth stood quite still. Only her breath came again. The wind brought it back to her, and as she drew it in, the step came near and David said again:

"Show me your face—your face; I have never seen your face."

She turned then, very slowly—in obedience to an effort, that left her drained of strength.

David was standing in the middle of the room. His feet were bare, as he had risen from his bed, but his eyes were open, and they looked not at, but through Elizabeth, to the place where she walked in his dream.

"Ah!" said David on a long, slow, sudden breath.

He came nearer—nearer. Now he stood beside her, and the wind swept suddenly between them, and eddying, drove a great swathe of her unfastened hair across his breast. David put up his hand and touched the hair.

"But I can't see your face," he said, in a strange, complaining note. "The moon shines on your hair, but not upon your face. Show me your face—your face—"

She moved, and the moon shone on her. Her face was as white as ivory. Her eyes wide and dark—as dark as the darkening sky. They stood in silence, and the moon sank low.

Then David put out his hands and touched her on the breast.

"Now I have seen your face," he said. "Now I am content because I have seen your face. I have gone hungry for the sight of it, and have gone thirsty for the love of you, and all the years I have never seen your face."

"And now—?"

Elizabeth's voice came in a whisper.

"Now I am content."

"Why?"

"Your face is the face of Love," said David Blake.

His hands still held her hair. They lay against her heart, and moved a little as she breathed.

A sudden terror raised its head and peered at Elizabeth. Mary—oh, God—if he took her for Mary. The thought struck her as with a spear of ice. It burned as ice burns, and froze her as ice freezes. Her lips were stiff as she forced out the words:

"Who am I? Say."

His hands were warm. He answered her at once.

"We are in the Dream, you and I. You are the Woman of the Dream. Your face is the face of Love, and your hair—your floating hair—" He paused.

"My hair—what colour is my hair?" whispered Elizabeth.

"Your hair—" He lifted a strand of it. The wind played through it, and it brushed his cheek, then fell again upon her breast. His hand closed down upon it.

"What colour is my hair?" said Elizabeth very quietly. Mary's hair would be dark. If he said dark hair, dark like the night which would close upon them when that low moon was gone—what should she do—oh, god, what should she do?

"Your hair is gold—moon gold, which is pale as a dream," said David Blake. And a great shudder ran through Elizabeth from head to foot as the ice went from her heart.

"Like moon gold," repeated David, and his hands were warm against her breast.

And then all at once they were in the dark together, for the moon went out suddenly like a blown candle. She had dropped into a bank of clouds that rose from the clouding west. The wind blew a little chill, and as suddenly as the light had gone, David, too, was gone. One moment, so near—touching her in the darkness—and the next, gone—gone noiselessly, leaving her shaking, quivering.

When she could move, she lit a candle and looked in through the open door. David lay upon his side, with one hand under his cheek. He was sleeping like a child.

Elizabeth shut the door.

CHAPTER XVIII

THE FACE OF LOVE

Where have I seen these tall black trees,
  Two and two and three—yes, seven,
Standing all about in a ring,
  And pointing up to Heaven?

Where have I seen this black, black pool,
  That never ruffles to any breath,
But stares and stares at the empty sky,
  As silently as death?

How did we come here, you and I,
  With the pool beneath, and the trees above?
Oh, even in death or the dusk of a dream,
  You are heart of the heart of Love.

ELIZABETH was very pale when she came down the next day. As she dressed, she could hear David singing and whistling in his room. He went down the stairs like a schoolboy, and when she followed she found him opening his letters and whistling still.

"Hullo!" he said. "Good-morning. You 're late, and I've only got half an hour to breakfast in. I 'm starving. I don't believe you gave me any dinner last night. I shall be late for lunch. Give me something cold when I come in, I've got a pretty full day—"

Elizabeth wondered as she listened to him if it were she who had dreamed.

That evening he looked up suddenly from his book and said:

"Was the moon full last night?"

"Not quite."

Elizabeth was startled. Did he, after all, remember anything?

"When is it full?"

"To-morrow, I think. Why?"

Her breathing quickened a little as she asked the question.

"Because I dreamed my dream again last night, and it generally comes when the moon is full," he said.

Elizabeth turned as if to get more light upon her book. She could not sit and let him see her face.

"Your dream—?"

Her voice was low.

"Yes."

He paused for so long that the silence seemed to close upon Elizabeth. Then he said thoughtfully:

"Dreams are odd things. I've had this one off and on since I was a boy. And it's always the same. But I have not had it for months. Then last night—" He broke off. "Do you know I've never told any one about it before—does it bore you?"

"No," said Elizabeth, and could not have said more to save her life.

"It's a queer dream, and it never varies. There's always the same long, wet stretch of sand, and the moon shining over the sea. And a woman—"

"Yes—"

"She stands at the edge of the sea with the moon behind her, and the wind—did I tell you about the wind?—it blows her hair and her dress. And I have never seen her face."

"No?"

"No, never. I've always wanted to, but I can never get near enough, and the moon is behind her. When I was a boy, I used to walk in my sleep when I had the dream. I used to wake up in all sorts of odd places. Once I got as far as the front-door step, and waked with my feet on the wet stones. I suppose I was looking for the Woman."

Elizabeth took a grip of herself.

"Do you walk in your sleep now?"

He shook his head.

"Oh, no. Not since I was a boy," he said cheerfully. "Mrs. Havergill would have evolved a ghost story long ago if I had."

"And last night your dream was just the same?"

"Yes, just the same. It always ends just when it might get exciting."

"Did you wake?"

"No. That's the odd part. One is supposed to dream only when one is waking, and of course it's very hard to tell, but my impression is, that at the point where my dream ends I drop more deeply asleep. Dreams are queer things. I don't know why I told you about this one."

He took up his book as he spoke, and they talked no more.

Elizabeth went to her room early that night, but she did not get into bed. She moved about the room, hanging up the dress she had worn, folding her things—even sorting out a drawer full of odds and ends. It seemed as if she must occupy herself.

Presently she heard David come up and go into his room. She went on rolling up stray bits of lace and ribbon with fingers that seemed oddly numb. When she had finished, she began to brush her hair, standing before the glass, and brushing with a long, rhythmic movement. After about ten minutes she turned suddenly and blew out the candle. She went to the window and opened it wide.

Then, because she was trembling, she sat down on the window-seat and waited. The night came into the room and filled it. The trees moved above the water. The rumble of traffic in the High Street sounded very far away. It had nothing to do with the world in which Elizabeth waited. There was no wind to-night. It was very still and warm. The moon shone.

When the door opened, Elizabeth knew that she had known that he would come. He crossed the room and took her in his arms. She felt his arms about her, she felt his kiss, and there was nothing of the unsubstantial stuff of dreams in his strong clasp. For one moment, as her lips kissed too, she thought that he was awake—that he had remembered, but as she stepped back and looked into his face she saw that he was in his dream. His eyes looked far away. Then he kissed her again, and dreaming or waking her soul went out of her and was his soul, her very consciousness was no more hers, but his, and she, too, saw that strange, moon-guarded shore, and she, too, heard the wind. But the night— the night was still. Where did it come from, this sudden rush of the wind, that seemed to blow through her? From far away it came, from very far away, and it passed through her and on to its own far place again, a rushing eddy of wind, whirling about some unknown centre.

Elizabeth was giddy and faint with the singing of that wind in her ears. The moon was in her eyes. She trembled, and hid them upon David's breast.

"David," she whispered at last, and he answered her.

"Love—love—"

She turned a little from the light and looked at him. There was a smile upon his face, and his eyes smiled too.

"Where are we?" she said. And David laid his face against hers and said:

"We are in the Dream."

"David, what is the Dream? Do you know? Tell me."

"It is the Dream," he said, "the old dream, the dream that has no waking."

"And who am I? Am I Elizabeth?" She feared so much to say it, and could not rest till it was said.

"Elizabeth." He repeated the word, and paused. His eyes clouded.

"You are the Woman of the Dream."

"But I have a name—"

"Yes—you have a name, but I have forgotten—if I could remember it. It is the name—the old name—the name you had before the moon went down. It was at night. You kissed me. There were so many trees. I knew your name. Then the moon went down, and it was dark, and I forgot—not you—only the name. Are you angry, love, because I have forgotten your name?"

There was trouble in his tone.

"No, not angry," said Elizabeth, with a quiver in her voice. "Will you call me Elizabeth, David? Will you say Elizabeth to me?"

He said "Elizabeth," and as he said it his face changed. For a moment she thought that he was waking. His arms dropped from about her, and he drew a long, deep breath that was like a sigh.

Then he went slowly from her into the darkness of his own room, walking as if he saw.

Elizabeth fell on her knees by the window-seat and hid her face. The wind still sang in her ears.

CHAPTER XIX

THE FULL MOON

The sun was cold, the dark dead Moon
  Hung low behind dull leaden bars,
And you came barefoot down the sky
  Between the grey unlighted Stars.

You laid your hand upon my soul,
  My soul that cried to you for rest,
And all the light of the lost Sun
  Was in the comfort of your breast.

There was no veil upon your heart,
  There was no veil upon your eyes;
I did not know the Stars were dim,
  Nor long for that dead Moon to rise.

THEY dined with Edward and Mary next day. The centipedes were still immured, and Edward made tentative overtures to David on the subject of broaching the case after dinner.

"Edward is the soul of hospitality," David said afterwards. "He keeps his best to the end. First a positively good dinner, then some comparatively enjoyable music, and, last of all, the superlatively enthralling centipedes."

At the time, he complied with a very good grace. He even contrived a respectable degree of enthusiasm when the subject came up.

It was Mary who insisted on the comparatively agreeable music.

"No—I will not have you two going off by yourselves the moment you've swallowed your dinner. It's not *good* for people. Edward will certainly have indigestion—yes, Edward, you know you will. Come and have coffee with us in a proper and decent fashion, and we'll have some music, and then you shall do anything you like, and I'll talk to Elizabeth."

Edward sang only one song, and then said that he was hoarse, which was not true. But Elizabeth was glad when the door closed upon him and David, for the song Edward had sung was the one thing on earth which she felt least able to hear. He sang, *O Moon of my Delight*, transposed by Mary to suit his voice, and he sang it with his usual tuneful correctness.

Elizabeth looked up only once, and that was just at the end. David was looking at her with a frown of perplexity. But as Edward remarked that he was hoarse, David passed his hand across his eyes for a moment, as if to brush something away, and rose with alacrity to leave the room.

When they were gone Mary drew a chair close to her sister and sat down. She was rather silent for a time, and Elizabeth was beginning to find it hard to keep her own thoughts at bay, when Mary said in a new, gentle voice:

"Liz, I 'm so *happy*."

"Are you, Molly?" She spoke rather absently, and Mary became softly offended.

"Don't you want to know why, Liz? I don't believe you care a bit. I don't believe you'd mind if I were ever so miserable, now that you've got David, and are happy yourself!"

Elizabeth came back to her surroundings.

"Oh, Molly, what a goose you are, and what a monster you make me out. What is it, Mollykins, tell me?"

"I've a great mind not to. I don't believe you really care. I wouldn't tell you a word, only I can't help it. Oh, Liz, I 'm going to have a baby, and I thought I never should. I was making myself *wretched* about it."

She caught Elizabeth's hand and squeezed it.

"Oh, Liz, be glad for me. I 'm so glad and happy, and I want some one to be glad too. You don't know how I've wanted it. No one knows. I've simply hated all the people in the *Morning Post* who had babies. I've not even read the first column for weeks, and when Sybil Delamere sent me an invitation to her baby's christening—she was married the same day I was, you know—I just tore it up and burnt it. And now it's really coming to me, and you 're to be glad for me, Liz."

"Molly, darling, I *am* glad—so glad."

"Really?"

Mary looked up into her sister's face, searchingly.

"You 're thinking of me, *really* of me—not about David, as you were just now? Oh, yes, I knew."

Elizabeth laughed.

"Really, Molly, mayn't I think of my own husband?"

"Not when I 'm telling you about a thing like this," said Mary. "Liz, you are the first person I have told, the very first."

Elizabeth did not allow her thoughts to wander again. As they talked, the rain beat heavily against the windows, and they heard the rush of it in the gutters below.

"What a pity," Mary cried. "How quickly it has come up, and last night was so lovely. Did you see the moon? And to-night it is full."

"Yes, to-night it is full," said Elizabeth.

Edward and Mary came down to see their guests off. Edward shut the door behind them.

"What a night!" he exclaimed. But Mary came close and whispered:

"I've told her."

"Have you?"

Edward's tone was just the least shade perfunctory. He slid home the bolt of the door and turning, caught Mary in his arms and hugged her.

"O Mary, *darling!*"

Mary glowed, responsive.

"O Mary, darling, it really is a new spider," he cried.

David and Elizabeth walked home in a steady downpour. Mary had lent her overshoes, and she had tucked up her dress under a mackintosh of Edward's. There was much merriment over their departure with a large umbrella between them, but as they walked home, they both grew silent. Elizabeth said good-night in the hall, and ran up to her room. To-night he would not come. Oh, to-night she felt quite sure that he would not come. It was dark. She heard the rain falling into the river, and she could just see how the trees bent in the rush of it. And yet she sat for an hour, by her window, in the dark, waiting breathlessly for that which would not happen.

The time went slowly by. The rain fell, and it was cold. Elizabeth lay down in the great square bed, and presently she slept, lulled by the steady dropping of the rain. She slept, and in her sleep she dreamed that she was sinking fathoms deep in a stormy, angry sea. Far overhead, she could hear the clash of the waves, and the long, long sullen roar of the swelling storm. And she went down and down into a black darkness that was deeper than any night—down, till she lost the roar of the storm above, down until all sound was gone, and she was alone in a black silence that would never lift or break again. Her soul was cold and blind, and most unendurably alone. Then something touched her, something that was warm. There came upon her that strange sense of home-coming, which comes to us in dreams, when love comes back to us across the sundering years, and all the pains of life, the pains of death, vanish and are gone, and we are come home—home to the place where we would be.

In her dream Elizabeth was come home. It was so long, so long, that she had wandered—so many years, so many lands—such weary feet and such a weary way. Now she was come home.

She stirred and opened her eyes. The rain had ceased. The room was dark, but the moon shone, for a single shaft struck between the curtains and lay above the bed like a silver feather dropped from some great passing wing.

Elizabeth was awake. She saw these things. She was come home. David's arms were about her in the darkness.

CHAPTER XX

THE WOMAN OF THE DREAM.

Oh, was it in the dead of night,
　　Or in the dark before the day;
You came to me and kneeling, knew
　　The thing that I would never say?

There was no star, nor any moon,
　　There was no light from pole to pole,
And yet you saw the secret thing,
　　That I had hid within my soul.

You saw the secret and the shrine,
　　You bowed your head and went your way—
Oh, was it in the dead of night,
　　Or in the dark that brings the day?

FOR the next fortnight Elizabeth lived in a dream from which she scarcely woke by day. The dream life—the dream love—the dream itself—these became her life. In the moments that came nearest the waking she trembled, because if the dream was her life, the waking would be death. But for the rest of the time she walked in a trance. Earth budded, and the birds built nests. The green of woodland places went down under a flood of bluebells. The children made cowslip balls. All day long the sun shone out of a blue sky, and at night David came to her. Always he came at night, and went away in the dawn. And he remembered nothing.

Once she put her face to his in the darkness, and said:

"Oh, David, won't you remember—won't you ever remember? Am I only the Woman of the Dream? When will you remember?"

Then David was troubled in his dream, and stirred and went from her an hour before the time of his going.

Towards the end of the fortnight her trance wore thin. It was then that everything she saw or read seemed to press in upon one sore spot. If she went to the Mottisfonts', there was Mary with her talk of Edward and the baby. Edward!—Elizabeth could have laughed; but the laughter went too. If there were not much of Edward, at least Mary had all that there was. And the child—did not she, too, desire children? But the child of a dream. How could she give to David the child of a dream already forgotten? If she walked, there were lovers in every lane, young lovers, who loved each other by day and in the eye of the sun. If she took up a book—once what she read was:

Come to me in my dreams, and then
By day I shall be well again!
For then the night will more than pay
The hopeless longing of the day.

and another time, Kingsley's *Dolcino to Margaret*. Then came a day when she opened her Bible and read:

"If a man walk in the night, he stumbleth, because there is no light in him."

That day she came broad awake. The daze passed from her. Her brain was clear, and her conscience—the inner vision rose before her, showing her an image troubled and confused. What had she done? And what was she doing now? Day by day David looked at her with the eyes of a friend, and night by night he came to her, the lover of a dream. Which was the reality? Which was the real David? If the David of the dream were real, conscious in sleep of some mysterious oneness, the sense of which was lost in the glare of day—then she could wait, and bear, and hope, till the realization was so strong that the sun might shine upon it and show to David awake what the sleeping David knew.

But if the David of the dream were not the real David, then what was she? Mistress and no wife—the mistress of a dream mood that never touched Reality at all.

Two scalding tears in Elizabeth's eyes—two and no more. The others burned her heart.

And the thought stayed with her.

That evening after dinner Elizabeth looked up from her embroidery. The silence had grown to be too full of thoughts. She could not bear it.

"What are you reading, David?" she asked.

He laughed and said:

"Sentimental poetry, ma'am. Would you have suspected me of it? I find it very soothing."

"Do you?"

She paused, and then said with a flutter in her throat:

"Do you ever write poetry now, David? You used to."

"Yes, I remember boring you with it."

He coloured a little as he spoke.

"But since then?"

"Oh, yes—"

"Show me some—"

"Not for the world."

"Why not?"

"Poetry is such an awful give away. How any one ever dares to publish any, I don't know. I suppose they get hardened. But one's most private letters aren't a patch on it. One puts down all one's grumbles, one's moonstruck fancies, the ravings of one's inanest moments. Mine are not for circulation, thanks."

Elizabeth did not laugh. Instead she said, quite seriously,

"David, I wish you would show me some of it."

He looked rather surprised, but got up, and presently came back with some papers in his hand, and threw them into her lap.

"There. There's one there that's rather odd. It's rotten poetry, but it gave me the oddest feelings when I wrote it. See if it does the same to you," and he laughed. There were three poems in Elizabeth's lap. The first was a vigorous bit of work—a ballad with a good ballad swing to it. Elizabeth read it and applauded.

"This is much better than your old things," she said, and he was manifestly pleased.

The next was a set of clever verses on a political topic of passing interest. Elizabeth laughed over it and laid it aside. Her thoughts were pleasantly diverted. Anything was welcome that brought her nearer to the David of the day.

She took up the third poem. It was called:

EGYPT

Egypt sands are burning hot,
  Burning hot and dry,
How they scorched us as we worked,
  Toiling, you and I,
When we built the Pyramid in Egypt.

Heaven like hammered brass above,
  Earth like brass below,
How the sweat of torment ran,
  All those years ago,
When we built the Pyramid in Egypt.

When the dreadful day was done,
  Night was like your eyes,
Sweet and cool and comforting—
  We were very wise,
When we built the Pyramid in Egypt.

We were very wise, my dear,
  Children, lovers, gods.
Where's the wisdom that we knew,
  With our world at odds,
When we built the Pyramid in Egypt?

Now your hand is strange to mine,
  Now you heed me not,
Life and death and love and pain,
  You have quite forgot,
You have quite forgotten me and Egypt.

I would bear it all again,
  Just to take your hand,
Bend my body to the whip,
  Tread the burning sand,
Build another Pyramid in Egypt.

Toiling, toiling, all the day;
  Loving you by night,
I'd go back three thousand years
  If I only might,—
Back to toil and pain and you and Egypt.

When she looked up at the end, David spoke at once.
"Well," he said, "what does it say to you?"

"I don't quite know."

"It set up one of those curious thought-waves. One seems to remember something out of an extraordinarily distant past. Have you ever felt it? I believe most people have. There are all sorts of theories to account for it. The two sides of the brain working unequally, and several others. But the impression is common enough, and the theories have been made to fit it. Of course the one that fits most happily is the hopelessly unscientific one of reincarnation. Well, my thought-wave took me back to Egypt and—"

He hesitated.

"Tell me."

Elizabeth's voice was eager.

"Oh, nothing."

"Yes, tell me."

He laughed at her earnestness.

"Well, then—I saw the woman's eyes."

"Yes."

"They were grey. That's all. And I thought it odd."

He broke off, and Elizabeth asked no more. She knew very well why he had thought it odd that the woman's eyes should be grey. The poems were dated, and *Egypt* bore the date of a year ago. He was in love with Mary then, and Mary's eyes were dark—dark hazel eyes.

That night she woke from a dream of Mary, and heard David whispering a name in his sleep, but she could not catch the name. The old shamed dread and horror came upon her, strong and unbroken. She slipped from bed, and stood by the window, panting for breath. And out of the darkness David called to her:

"Love, where are you gone to?"

If he would say her name—if he would only say her name. She had no words to answer him, but she heard him rise and come to her.

"Why did you go away?" he said, touching her. And as she had done once before, Elizabeth cried out.

"Who am I, David?—tell me! Am I Mary?"

He repeated the name slowly, and each repetition was a wound.

"Mary," he said, wonderingly, "there is no Mary in the Dream. There are only you and I—and you are Love—"

"And if I went out of the Dream?" said Elizabeth, leaning against his breast. The comfort of his touch stole back into her heart. Her breathing steadied.

"Then I would come and find you," said David Blake.

It was the next day that Agneta's letter came. Elizabeth opened it at breakfast and exclaimed.

"What is it?"

She lifted a face of distress.

"David, should you mind if I were to go away for a little? Agneta wants me."

"Agneta?"

"Yes, Agneta Mainwaring. You remember, I used to go and stay with the Mainwarings in Devonshire."

"Yes, I remember. What's the matter with her?"

"She is engaged to Douglas Strange, the explorer, and there are—rumours that his whole party has been massacred. He was working across Africa. She wants me to come to her. I think I must. You don't mind, do you?"

"No, of course not. When do you want to go?"

"I should like to go to-day. I could send her a wire," said Elizabeth. "I hope it's only a rumour, and not true, but I must go."

David nodded.

"Don't take it too much to heart, that's all," he said.

He said good-bye to her before he went out, told her to take care of herself, asked her to write, and inquired if she wanted any money.

When he had gone, Elizabeth told herself that this was the end of the Dream. She could drift no more with the tide of that moon-watched sea. She must think things out and come to some decision. Hitherto, if she thought by day, the night with its glamour threw over her thoughts a rainbow mist that hid and confused them. Now Agneta needed her, there would be work for her to do. And she would not see David again until she could look her conscience in the face.

CHAPTER XXI

ELIZABETH BLAKE

Oh, that I had wings, yea wings like a dove,
  Then would I flee away and be at rest;
Lo, the dove hath wings because she is a dove,
  God gave her wings and bade her build her nest,
Thy wings are stronger far, strong wings of love,
  Thy home is sure in His unchanging rest.

ELIZABETH went up to London by the 12.22, which is a fast train, and only stops once. She found Agneta, worn, tired, and cross.

"Thank Heaven, you've come, Lizabeth," she said. "All my relations have been to see me. They are so kind. They are so *dread*fully kind, and they all talk about its being God's Will, and tell me what a beautiful thing resignation is. If I believed in a God who arranged for people to murder each other in order to give some one else a moral lesson, I'd shoot myself. I really would And resignation is a perfectly horrible thing. I do think I must be getting a little better than I used to be, because I wasn't even rude to Aunt Henrietta, who told me I ought not to repine, because all was for the best. She said there were many trials in the married state, and that those who did not marry were spared the sorrow of losing a child or having an unfaithful husband. I really wasn't rude to her, Lizabeth—I swear I wasn't. But when I saw my cousin, Mabel Aston, coming up the street—you always can see her a mile off—I told Jane to say that I was very sorry, but I really couldn't see any one. Mabel won't ever forgive me, because all the other relations will tell her that I saw them. I told them every one that I was perfectly certain that Douglas was all right. And so I am. Yes, really. But, oh, Lizabeth, how I do hate the newspapers."

"I shouldn't read them," said Elizabeth.

"I don't! Nothing would induce me to. But I can't stop my relations from quoting reams of them, verbatim. By the by, do you mind dining at seven to-night? I want to go to church. I don't want you or Louis to come. Heavens, Lizabeth, you've no idea what a relief it is not to have to be polite, and say you want people when you don't."

When Agneta had gone out Elizabeth talked to Louis for a little, and then read. Presently she stopped reading and leaned back with closed eyes, thinking first of Agneta, then of herself and David. Louis's voice broke in upon her thoughts.

"Lizabeth, what *is* it?"

She was startled.

"Oh, I was just thinking."

He frowned.

"What is the good?" he said. "I told you I could see. You 're troubled, horribly troubled about something. And it's not Agneta. What is it?"

Elizabeth was rather pale.

"Oh, Louis," she said, "please don't. I'd rather you didn't. And it's not what you think. It's not really a trouble. I 'm puzzled. I don't know what to do. There's something I have to think out. And it's not clear—I can't quite see—"

Louis regarded her seriously.

"If any man lack wisdom," he said. "That's a pretty good thing in the pike-staff line. Good Lord, fancy me preaching to you. It's amusing, isn't it?"

He laughed a little.

Elizabeth nodded.

"You can go on," she said.

He considered.

"I don't know that I've got anything more to say except that—things that puzzle one—there's always the touchstone of reality. And things one doesn't want to do because they're difficult, or because they hurt, or because they take us away from something we've set our heart on—well—if they're right, they're right, and there's an end of it. And the right thing, well, it's the best thing all round. And when we get where we can see it properly, it's—well, it's trumps all right."

Elizabeth nodded again. "Thank you, Louis," she said. "I've been shirking. I think I've known it all along. Only when one shirks, it's part of it to wrap oneself up in a sort of mist, and call everything by a wrong name. I've got to change my labels . . ."

Her voice died away, and they sat silent until Agneta's key was heard in the latch. She came in looking rested.

"Nice church?" said Elizabeth.

"Yes," said Agneta, "very nice. I feel better."

During the week that followed, Elizabeth had very little time to spare for her own concerns, and Agneta clung to her and clung to hope, and day by day the hope grew fainter. It was the half-hours when they waited for the telephone bell to ring that brought the grey threads into Agneta's hair. Twice daily Louis rang up, and each time, after the same agonizing suspense, came the same message, "No news yet." Towards the end of the week, there was a wire to say that a rumour had reached the coast that Mr. Strange was alive and on his way down the river.

It was then that Agneta broke down. Whilst all had despaired, she had held desperately to hope, but when Louis followed his message home, he found Agneta with her head in Elizabeth's lap, weeping slow, hopeless tears.

Then, forty-eight hours later, Douglas Strange himself cabled in code to say that he had abandoned part of his journey owing to a native rising, and was returning at once to England.

"And now, Lizabeth," said Agneta, "now your visit begins, please. This hasn't been a visit, it has been purgatory. I 'm sure we've both expiated all the sins we've ever committed or are likely to commit. Louis, take the receiver off that brute of a telephone. I shall *never*, *never* hear a telephone bell again without wanting to scream. Lizabeth, let's go to a music hall."

Next day Agneta said suddenly:

"Lizabeth, what is it?"

"What is what?"

Agneta's little dark face became serious.

"Lizabeth, I've been a beast. I've only been thinking about myself. Now it's your turn. What's the matter?"

Elizabeth was silent.

"Mayn't I ask? Do you mind?"

Elizabeth shook her head.

"Which is the 'no' for?"

"Both," said Elizabeth.

"I mustn't ask then. You'd rather not talk about it? Really?"

"Yes, really, Neta, dear."

"Right you are."

Agneta was silent for a few minutes. They were sitting together in the firelight, and she watched the play of light and shade upon Elizabeth's face. It was beautiful, but troubled.

"Lizabeth, you used not to be beautiful, but you are beautiful now," she said suddenly.

"Am I?"

"Yes, I always loved your face, but it wasn't really beautiful. Now I think it is."

"Anything else?" Elizabeth laughed a little.

"Yes, the patient look has gone. You used to look so patient that it *hurt*. As if you were carrying a heavy load and just knew you had got to carry it without making any fuss."

"Issachar, in fact—"

"No, not then, but I 'm not so sure now. I *think* there *are* two burdens now."

Elizabeth laid her hand on Agneta's lips.

"Agneta, you ought to be ashamed of yourself. Stop thought-reading this very minute. I never gave you leave."

"Sorry." Agneta kissed the hand against her lips and laid it back in Elizabeth's lap. "Oh, Lizabeth, *why* didn't you marry Louis?" she said, and Elizabeth saw that her eyes were full of tears. The firelight danced on a brilliant, falling drop.

"Because I love David," said Elizabeth. "And love is worth while, Agneta. It is very well worth while. You knew it was when you thought that Douglas was dead. Would you have gone back to a year ago?"

"Ah, Lizabeth, don't," said Agneta.

She leaned her head against Elizabeth's knee and was still.

All that week, Elizabeth slept little and thought much. And her thought was prayer. She did not kneel when she prayed, and she had her own idea of what prayer should be. Not petition. The Kingdom of Heaven is about us. We have but to open our eyes and take what is our own. Therefore not petition. What Elizabeth called prayer was far more like taking something out of the darkness, to look at it in the light. And before the light, all things evil, all things that were not good and not of God, vanished and were not. If thine eye be single, thy whole body shall be full of light. In this manner, David's sleeplessness had been changed to rest and healing, and in this same manner, Elizabeth now knew that she must test the strange dream-state in which David loved her. And in her heart of hearts she did not think that it would stand the test. She believed that, subjected to this form of prayer, the dream would vanish and she be left alone.

She faced the probability, and facing it, she prayed for light, for wisdom, for the Reality that annihilates the shadows of man's thought. When she used words at all, they were the words of St. Patrick's prayer:

I bind to myself to-day,
The Power of God to protect me,
The Might of God to uphold me,
The Wisdom of God to guide me,
The Light of God to shine upon me,
The Love of God to encompass me.

During these days Agneta looked at her anxiously, but she asked no questions at all, and Elizabeth loved her for it.

Elizabeth went home on the 15th of June. After hard struggle, she had come into a place of clear vision. If the dream stood the test, if in spite of all her strivings towards Truth, David still came to her, she would take the dream to be an earnest of some future waking. If the dream ceased, if David came no more, then she must cast her bread of love upon the waters of the Infinite, God only knowing, if after many days, she should be fed.

David was very much pleased to have her back. He told her so with a laugh—confessed that he had missed her.

When Elizabeth went to her room that night, she sat down on the window-seat and watched. It had rained, but the night was clear again. She looked from the window, and the midsummer beauty slid into her soul. The rain had washed the sky to an unearthly translucent purity, but out of the west streamed a radiance of turquoise light. It filled the night, and as it mounted towards the zenith, the throbbing colour passed by imperceptible degrees into a sapphire haze. The horizon was a ghostly line of far, pure emerald. This transfiguring glow had all the sunset's fire, only there was neither red nor gold in it. The ether itself flamed, and the colour of that flame was blue. It was the light of vision, the very light of a Midsummer's Dream. The cloud that had shed the rain brooded apart with wings of folded gloom. Two or three drifting feathers of dark grey vapour barred the burning blue. Perishably fine, they dissolved against the glow, and one amazing star showed translucent at the vapour's edge, now veiled, now blazing out as the mist wavered and withdrew from so much brightness. A night for love, a night for lovers' dreams.

Yearning came upon Elizabeth like a flood. Just once more to see him look at her with love. Just once more—once more, to feel his arms, his kiss—to weep upon his breast and say farewell.

She put her hand out waveringly until it touched the wall. She shut her eyes against the beauty of the night, and strove with the longing that rent her. Her lips framed broken words. She said them over and over again until the tumult died in her, and she was mistress of her thoughts. Immortal love could never lose by Truth.

Now she could look again upon the night. The trees were very black. The wind stirred them. The sky was full of light made mystical. Which of the temples that man has built, has light for its walls, and cloud and fire for its pillars? In which of them has the sun his tabernacle, through which of them does the moon pass, by a path of silver adoration? What altar is served by the rushing winds and lighted by the stars? In all the temples that man has made, man bows his head and worships, but in the Temple of the Universe it is the Heavens themselves that declare the Glory of God.

Elizabeth's thought rose up and up. In the divine peace it rested and was stilled.

And David did not come.

CHAPTER XXII

AFTER THE DREAM

In Him we live, He is our Source, our Spring,
    And we, His fashioning.
We have no sight except by His foreseeing,
    In Him we live and move and have our being,
He spake the Word, and lo! Creation stood,
    And God said, It is good.

DAVID came no more. The dream was done. During the summer days there rang continually in Elizabeth's ears the words of a song—one of Christina's wonderful songs that sing themselves with no other music at all.

    The hope I dreamed of was a dream
        Was but a dream, and now I wake
    Exceeding comfortless, and worn, and old,
        For a dream's sake.

"Exceeding comfortless." Yes, there were hours when that was true. She had taken her heart and broken it for Truth's sake, and the broken thing cried aloud of its hurt. Only by much striving could she still it and find peace.

The glamour of the June days was gone too. July was a wet and stormy month, and Elizabeth was thankful for the rain and the cold, at which all the world was grumbling.

Mary came in one July day with a face that matched the weather.

"Why, Molly," said Elizabeth, kissing her, "what's the matter, child?"

Mary might have asked the same question, but she was a great deal too much taken up with her own affairs.

"Edward and I have quarreled," she said with a sob in the words, and sitting down, she burst into uncontrollable tears.

"But what is it all about?" asked Elizabeth, with her arm around her sister. "Molly, do hush. It is so bad for you. What has Edward done?"

"Men are brutes," declared Mary.

"Now, I 'm sure Edward isn't," returned Elizabeth, with real conviction.

Mary sat up.

"He is," she declared. "No, Liz, just listen. It was all over baby's name."

"What, already?"

"Well, of course, one plans things. If one doesn't, well, there was Dorothy Jackson—don't you remember? She was very ill, and the baby had to be christened in a hurry, because they didn't think it was going to live. And nobody thought the name mattered, so the clergyman just gave it the first name that came into his head, and the baby didn't die after all, and when Dorothy found she'd got to go through life with a daughter called Harriet, she very nearly died all over again. So, you see, one has to think of things. So I had thought of a whole lot of names, and last night I said to Edward, 'What shall we call it?' and he looked awfully pleased and said, 'What do you think?' And I said, 'What would you like best?' And he said, 'I'd like it to be called after you, Mary, darling. I got Jack

Webster's answer to-day, and he says I may call it anything I like.' Well, of *course*, I didn't see what it had to do with Jack Webster, but I thought Edward must have asked him to be godfather. I was rather put out. I didn't think it quite *nice* beforehand, you know."

The bright colour of indignation had come into Mary's cheeks, and she spoke with great energy.

"Of *course*, I just thought that, and then Edward said, 'So it shall be called after you—Arachne Mariana.' I thought what *hideous* names, but all I said was, 'Oh, darling, but I want a boy'; and do you know, Liz, Edward had been talking about a spider all the time—the spider that Jack Webster sent him. I don't believe he cares nearly as much for the baby, I really don't, and I wish I was *dead*."

Mary sobbed afresh, and it took Elizabeth a good deal of the time to pacify her.

Mrs. Havergill brought in tea, it being Sarah's afternoon out. When she was taking away the tea-things, after Mary had gone, she observed:

"Mrs. Mottisfont, she do look pale, ma'am."

"Mrs. Mottisfont is going to have a baby," said Elizabeth, smiling.

Mrs. Havergill appeared to dismiss Mary's baby with a slight wave of the hand.

"I 'ad a cousin as 'ad twenty-three," she observed in tones of lofty detachment.

"Not all at once?" said Elizabeth faintly.

Mrs. Havergill took no notice of this remark.

"Yes, twenty-three, pore soul. And when she wasn't 'aving of them, she was burying of them. Ten she buried, and thirteen she reared, and many's the time I've 'eard 'er say, she didn't know which was the most trouble."

She went out with the tray, and later, when Sarah had returned, she repeated Mrs. Blake's information in tones of sarcasm.

"'There's to be a baby at the Mottisfonts',' she says, as if I didn't know that. And I says, 'Yes, ma'am,' and that's all as passed."

Mrs. Havergill had a way of forgetting her own not inconsiderable contributions to a conversation.

"'Yes, ma'am,' I says, expecting every moment as she'd up and say, 'and one 'ere, too, Mrs. Havergill,' but no, not a blessed word, and me sure of it for weeks. But there—they're all the same with the first, every one's to be blind and deaf. All the same, Sarah, my girl, if she don't want it talked about, she don't, so just you mind and don't talk, not if she don't say nothing till the christening's ordered."

When Elizabeth knew that she was going to have a child, her first thought was, "Now, I must tell David," and her next, "How can I tell him, how can I possibly tell him?" She lay on her bed in the darkness and faced the situation. If she told David, and he did not believe her—that was possible, but not probable. If she told him, and he believed her as to the facts—but believed also that this strange development was due in some way to some influence of hers—conscious or unconscious hypnotism—the thought broke off half-way. If he believed this—and it was likely that he would believe it—Elizabeth covered her eyes with her hand. Even the darkness was no shield. How should she meet David's eyes in the light, if he were to believe this? What would he think of her? What must he think of her? She began to weep slow tears of shame and agony. What was she to do? To wait until some accident branded her in David's eyes, or to go to him with a most unbelievable tale? She tried to find words that she could say, and she could find none. Her flesh shrank, and she knew that she could not do it. There were no words. The tears ran slowly, very slowly, between her fingers. Elizabeth was cold. The room was full of the empty dark. All the world was dark and empty too. She lay quite still for a very long time. Then there came upon her a curious gradual sense of companionship. It grew continually. At the last, she took her hands from before her face and opened her eyes. And there was a light in the room. It shed no glow on anything—it was just a light by itself. A steady, golden light. It was not moonlight, for there was no moon. Elizabeth lay and looked at it. It was very radiant and very soft. She ceased to weep and she ceased to be troubled. She knew with a certainty that never faltered again, that she and David were one. Whether he would become conscious of their oneness during the space of this short mortal dream, she did not know, but it had ceased to matter. The thing that had tormented her was her own doubt. Now that was stilled for ever—Love walked again among the realities, pure and unashamed. The things of Time—the mistakes, the illusions, the shadows of Time—moved in a little misty dream, that could not touch her. Elizabeth turned on her side. She was warm and she was comforted.

She slept.

CHAPTER XXIII

ELIZABETH WAITS

And they that have seen and heard,
    Have wrested a gift from Fate
That no man taketh away.
    For they hold in their hands the key,
To all that is this-side Death,
    And they count it as dust by the way,
As small dust, driven before the breath
    Of Winds that blow to the day.

"DO you remember my telling you about my dream?" said David, next day. He spoke quite suddenly, looking up from a letter that he was writing.

"Yes, I remember," said Elizabeth. She even smiled a little.

"Well, it was so odd—I really don't know what made me think of it just now, but it happened to come into my head—do you know that I dreamt it every night for about a fortnight? That was in May. I have never done such a thing before. Then it stopped again quite suddenly, and I haven't dreamt it since. I wonder whether speaking of it to you—" he broke off.

"I wonder," said Elizabeth.

"You see it came again and again. And the strange part was that I used to wake in the morning feeling as if there was a lot more of it. A lot more than there used to be. Things I couldn't remember—I don't know why I tell you this."

"It interests me," said Elizabeth.

"You know how one forgets a dream, and then, quite suddenly, you just don't remember it. It's the queerest thing—something gets the impression, but the brain doesn't record it. It's most amazingly provoking. Just now, while I was writing to Fossett, bits of something came over me like a flash. And now it's gone again. Do you ever dream?"

"Sometimes," said Elizabeth.

This was her time to tell him. But Elizabeth did not tell him. It seemed to her that she had been told, quite definitely, to wait, and she was dimly aware of the reason. The time was not yet.

David finished his letter. Then he said:

"Don't you want to go away this summer?"

"No," said Elizabeth, a little surprised. "I don't think I do. Why?"

"Most people seem to go away. Mary would like you to go with her, wouldn't she?"

"Yes, but I've told her I don't want to go. She won't be alone, you know, now that Edward finds that he can get away."

David laughed.

"Poor old Edward," he said. "A month ago this business couldn't get on without him. He was conscience-ridden, and snatched exiguous half-hours for Mary and his beetles. And now it appears, that after all, the business can get on without him. I don't know quite how Macpherson brought that fact home to Edward. He must have put it very straight, and I 'm afraid that Edward's feelings were a good deal hurt. Personally, I should say that the less Edward interferes with Macpherson the more radiantly will bank-managers smile upon Edward. Edward is a well-meaning person. Mr. Mottisfont would have called him damn well-meaning. And you cannot damn any man deeper than that in business. No, Edward can afford to take a holiday better than most people. He will probably start a marine collection and be perfectly happy. Why don't you join them for a bit?"

"I don't think I want to," said Elizabeth. "I 'm going up to London for Agneta's wedding next week. I don't want to go anywhere else. Do you want to get rid of me?"

To her surprise, David coloured.

"I?" he said. For a moment an odd expression passed across his face. Then he laughed.

"I might have wanted to flirt with Miss Dobell."

Agneta Mainwaring was married at the end of July.

"It's going to be the most awful show," she wrote to Elizabeth. "Douglas and I spend all our time trying to persuade each other that it isn't going to be awful, but we know it is. All our relations and all our friends, and all their children and all their best clothes, and an amount of fuss, worry, and botheration calculated to drive any one crazy. If I hadn't an enormous amount of self-control I should bolt, either with or without Douglas. Probably without him. Then he'd have a really thrilling time tracking me down. It's an awful temptation, and if you don't want me to give way to it, you'd better come up at least three days beforehand, and clamp on to me. Do come, Lizabeth. I really want you."

Elizabeth went up to London the day before the wedding, and Agneta detached herself sufficiently from her own dream to say:

"You 're not Issachar any longer. What has happened?"

"I don't quite know," said Elizabeth. "I don't think the burden's gone, but I think that some one else is carrying it for me. I don't seem to feel it any more."

Agneta smiled a queer little smile of understanding. Then she laughed.

"Good Heavens, Lizabeth, if any one heard us talking, how perfectly mad they would think us."

Elizabeth found August a very peaceful month. A large number of her friends and acquaintances were away. There were no calls to be paid and no notes to be written. She and David were more together than they had been since the time in Switzerland, and she was happy with a strange brooding happiness, which was not yet complete, but which awaited completion. She thought a great deal about the child—the child of the Dream. She came to think of it as an indication that behind the Dream was the Real.

Mary came back on the 15th of September. She was looking very well, and was once more in a state of extreme contentment with Edward and things in general. When she had poured forth a complete catalogue of all that they had done, she paused for breath, and looked suddenly and sharply at Elizabeth.

"Liz," she said. "Why, Liz."

To Elizabeth's annoyance, she felt herself colouring.

"Liz, and you never told me. Tell me at once. Is it true? Why didn't you tell me before?"

"Oh, Molly, what an Inquisitor you would have made!"

"Then it is true. And I suppose you told Agneta weeks ago?"

"I haven't told any one," said Elizabeth.

"Not Agneta? And I suppose if I hadn't guessed you wouldn't have told me for ages and ages and ages. Why didn't you tell me, Liz?"

"Why, I thought I'd wait till you came back, Molly."

Mary caught her sister's hand.

"Liz, aren't you glad? Aren't you pleased? Doesn't it make you happy? Oh, Liz, if I thought you were one of those *dreadful* women who don't want to have a baby, I—I don't know what I should do. I wanted to tell everybody. But then I was pleased. I don't believe you 're a bit *pleased*. Are you?"

"I don't know that pleased is exactly the word," said Elizabeth. She looked at Mary and laughed a little.

"Oh, Molly, do stop being Mrs. Grundy."

Mary lifted her chin.

"Just because I was interested," she said. "I suppose you'd rather I didn't care."

Then she relaxed a little.

"Liz, I 'm frightfully excited. Do be pleased and excited too. Why are you so stiff and odd? Isn't David pleased?"

She had looked away, but she turned quickly at the last words, and fixed her eyes on Elizabeth's face. And for a moment Elizabeth had been off her guard.

Mary exclaimed.

"Isn't he pleased? Doesn't he know? Liz, you don't mean to tell me—"

"I don't think you give me much time to tell you anything, Molly," said Elizabeth.

"He doesn't know? Liz, what's happened to you? Why are you so extraordinary? It's the sort of thing you read about in an early Victorian novel. Do you mean to say that you *really* haven't told David? That he doesn't know?"

Elizabeth's colour rose.

"Molly, my dear, do you think it is your business?" she said.

"Yes, I do," said Mary. "I suppose you won't pretend you 're not my own sister. And I think you must be quite mad, Liz. I do, indeed, You ought to tell David at once—at once. I can't *imagine* what Edward would have said if he had not known at once. You ought to go straight home and tell him now. Married people ought to be one. They ought never to have secrets."

Mary poured the whole thing out to Edward the same evening.

"I really don't know what has happened to Elizabeth," she said. "She is quite changed. I can't understand her at all. I think it is quite wicked of her. If she doesn't tell David soon, some one else ought to tell him."

Edward moved uneasily in his chair.

"People *don't* like being interfered with," he said.

"Well, I 'm sure nobody could call me an interfering person," said Mary. "It isn't interfering to be fond of people. If I weren't fond of Liz, I shouldn't care how strangely she behaved. I do think it's very strange of her—and I don't care what you say, Edward. I think David ought to be told. How would you have liked it if I'd hidden things from you?"

Edward rumpled up his hair.

"People don't like being interfered with," he said again.

At this Mary burst into tears, and continued to weep until Edward had called himself a brute sufficiently often to justify her contradicting him.

Elizabeth continued to wait. She was not quite as untroubled as she had been. The scene with Mary had brought the whole world of other people's thoughts and judgments much nearer. It was a troubling world. One full of shadows and perplexities. It pressed upon her a little and vexed her peace.

The days slid by. They had been pleasant days for David, too. For some time past he had been aware of a change in himself—a ferment. His old passion for Mary was dust. He looked back upon it now, and saw it as a delirium of the senses, a thing of change and fever. It was gone. He rejoiced in his freedom and began to look forward to the time when he and Elizabeth would enter upon a married life grounded upon friendship, companionship, and good fellowship. He had no desire to fall in love with Elizabeth, to go back to the old storms of passion and unrest. He cared a good deal for Elizabeth. When she was his wife he would care for her more deeply, but still on the same lines. He hoped that they would have children. He was very fond of children. And then, after he had planned it all out in his own mind, he became aware of the change, the ferment. What he felt did not come into the plan at all. He disliked it and he distrusted it, but none the less the change went on, the ferment grew. It was as if he had planned to walk on a clear, wide upland, under a still, untroubled air. In his own mind he had a vision of such a place. It was a place where a man might walk and be master of himself, and then suddenly—the driving of a mighty wind, and he could not tell from whence it came, or whither it went. The wind bloweth where it listeth. In those September days the wind blew very strongly, and as it blew, David came slowly to the knowledge that he loved Elizabeth. It was a love that seemed to rise in him from some great depth. He could not have told when it began. As the days passed, he wondered sometimes whether it had not been there always, deep amongst the deepest springs of thought and will. There was no fever in it. It was a thing so strong and sane and wholesome that, after the first wonder, it seemed to him to be a part of himself, a part which, missing, he had lost balance and mental poise.

He spoke to Elizabeth as usual, but he looked at her with new eyes. And he, too, waited.

He came home one day to find the household in a commotion. It appeared that Sarah had scalded her hand, Elizabeth was out, and Mrs. Havergill was divided between the rival merits of flour, oil, and a patent preparation which she had found very useful when suffering from chilblains. She safe-guarded her infallibility by remarking, that there was some as held with one thing and some as held with another. She also observed, that "scalds were 'orrid things."

"Now, there was an 'ousemaid I knew, Milly Clarke her name was, she scalded her hand very much the same as you 'ave, Sarah, and first thing, it swelled up as big as my two legs and arter that it turned to blood-poisoning, and the doctors couldn't do nothing for her, pore girl."

At this point Sarah broke into noisy weeping and David arrived. When he had bound up the hand, consoled the trembling Sarah, and suggested that she should have a cup of tea, he inquired where Elizabeth was. She might be at Mrs. Mottisfont's, suggested Mrs. Havergill, as she followed him into the hall.

"You 're not thinking of sending Sarah to the 'orspital, are you sir?"

"No, of course not, she'll be all right in a day or two. I'll just walk up the hill and meet Mrs. Blake."

"I 'm sure it's a mercy she were out," said Mrs. Havergill.

"Why?" said David, turning at the door. Mrs. Havergill assumed an air of matronly importance.

"It might ha' given her a turn," she said, "for the pore girl did scream something dreadful. I 'm sure it give me a turn, but that's neither here nor there. What I was thinking of was Mrs. Blake's condition, sir."

Mrs. Havergill was obviously a little nettled at David's expression.

"Nonsense," said David quickly.

Mrs. Havergill went back to Sarah.

"'Nonsense,' he says, and him a doctor. Why, there was me own pore mother as died with her ninth, and all along of a turn she got through seeing a child run over. And he says, 'Nonsense.'"

David walked up the hill in a state of mind between impatience and amusement. How women's minds did run on babies. He supposed it was natural, but there were times when one could dispense with it.

He found Mary at home and alone. "Elizabeth? Oh, no, she hasn't been near me for days," said Mary. "As it happened, I particularly *wanted* to see her. But she hasn't been near me."

She considered that Elizabeth was neglecting her. Only that morning she had told Edward so.

"She doesn't come to see me *on purpose*," she had said. "But I know quite well why. I don't at all approve of the way she's going on, and she knows it. I don't think it's *right*. I think some one ought to tell David. No, Edward, I really do. I don't understand Elizabeth at all, and she's simply afraid to come and see me because she knows that I shall speak my mind."

Now, as she sat and talked to David, the idea that it might be her duty to enlighten him presented itself to her mind afresh. A sudden and brilliant idea came into her head, and she immediately proceeded to act upon it.

"I had a special reason for wanting to see her," she said. "I had a lovely box of things down from town on approval, and I wanted her to see them."

"Things?" said David.

"Oh, clothes," said Mary, with a wave of the hand. "You now they'll send you anything now. By the way, I bought a present for Liz, though she doesn't *deserve* it. Will you take it down to her? I'll get it if you don't mind waiting a minute."

She was away for five minutes, and then returned with a small brown-paper parcel in her hand.

"You can open it when you get home," she said. "Open it and show it to Liz, and see whether you like it. Tell her I sent it with my love."

"Now there won't be any more nonsense," she told Edward.

Edward looked rather unhappy, but, warned by previous experience, said nothing,

David found Elizabeth in the dining-room. She was putting a large bunch of scarlet gladioli into a brown jug upon the mantelpiece.

"I've got a present for you," said David.

"David, how nice of you. It's not my birthday."

"I 'm afraid it's not from me at all. I looked in to see if you were with Mary, and she sent you this, with her love. By the way, you'd better go and see her, I think she's rather huffed."

As he spoke he was undoing the parcel. Elizabeth had her back towards him. The flowers would not stand up just as she wished them to.

"I can't think why Molly should send me a present," she said, and then all at once something made her turn round.

The brown-paper wrapping lay on the table. David had taken something white out of the parcel. He held it up and they both looked at it. It was a baby's robe, very fine, and delicately embroidered.

Elizabeth made a wavering step forward. The light danced on the white robe, and not only on the robe. All the room was full of small dancing lights. Elizabeth put her hand behind her and felt for the edge of the mantelpiece. She could not find it. Everything was shaking. She swung half round, and all the dancing lights flashed in her eyes as she fell forwards.

CHAPTER XXIV

THE LOST NAME

You are as old as Egypt, and as young as yesterday,
   Oh, turn again and look again, for when you look I know
The dusk of death is but a dream, that dreaming, dies away
   And leaves you with the lips I loved, three thousand years ago.

The mists of that forgotten dream, they fill your brooding eyes,
   With veil on strange revealing veil that wavers, and is gone,
And still between the veiling mists, the dim, dead centuries rise,
   And still behind the farthest veil, your burning soul burns on.

You are as old as Egypt, and as young as very Youth,
   Before your still, immortal eyes the ages come and go,
The dusk of death is but a dream that dims the face of Truth—
   Oh, turn again, and look again, for when you look, I know.

WHEN Elizabeth came to herself, the room was full of mist. Through the mist, she saw David's face, and quite suddenly in these few minutes it had grown years older.

He spoke. He seemed a long way off.

"Drink this."

"What is it?" said Elizabeth faintly.

"Water."

Elizabeth raised herself a little and drank. The faintness passed. She became aware that the collar of her dress was unfastened, and she sat up and began to fasten it.

David got up, too.

"I am all right."

There was no mist before Elizabeth's eyes now. They saw clearly, quite, quite clearly. She looked at David, and David's face was grey—old and grey. So it had come. Now in this hour of physical weakness. The thing she dreaded.

To her own surprise, she felt no dread now. Only a great weariness. What could she say? What was she to say? All seemed useless—not worth while. But then there was David's face, his grey, old face. She must do her best—not for her own sake, but for David's.

She wondered a little that it should hurt him so much. It was not as though he loved her, or had ever loved her. Only of course this was a thing to cut a man, down to the very quick of his pride and his self-respect. It was that—of course it was that.

Whilst she was thinking, David spoke. He was standing by the table fingering the piece of string that lay there.

"Elizabeth, do you know why you fainted?" he said.

"Yes," said Elizabeth, and said no more.

A sort of shudder passed over David Blake.

"Then it's true," he said in a voice that was hardly a voice at all. There was a sound, and there were words. But it was not like a man speaking. It was like a long, quick breath of pain.

"Yes," said Elizabeth. "It is true, David."

There was a very great pity in her eyes.

"Oh, my God!" said David, and he sat down by the table and put his head in his hands. "Oh, my God!" he said again.

Elizabeth got up. She was trembling just a little, but she felt no faintness now. She put one hand on the mantelpiece, and so stood, waiting.

There was a very long silence, one of those profound silences which seem to break in upon a room and fill it. They overlie and blot out all the little sounds of every-day life and usage. Outside, people came and went, the traffic in the High Street came and went, but neither to David, nor to Elizabeth, did there come the smallest sound. They were enclosed in a silence that seemed to stretch unbroken, from one Eternity to another. It became an unbearable torment. To his dying day, when any one spoke of hell, David glimpsed a place of eternal silence, where anguish burned for ever with a still unwavering flame.

He moved at last, slowly, like a man who has been in a trance. His head lifted. He got up, resting his weight upon his hands. Then he straightened himself. All his movements were like those of a man who is lifting an intolerably heavy load.

"Why did you marry me?" he asked in a tired voice and then his tone hardened. "Who is the man? Who is he? Will he marry you if I divorce you?"

An unbearable pang of pity went through Elizabeth, and she turned her head sharply. David stopped looking at her.

She to be ashamed—oh, God!—Elizabeth ashamed—he could not look at her. He walked quickly to the window. Then turned back again because Elizabeth was speaking.

"David," she said, in a low voice, "David, what sort of woman am I?"

A groan burst from David.

"You are a good woman. That's just the damnable part of it. There are some women, when they do a thing like this, one only says they've done after their kind—they're gone where they belong. When a good woman does it, it's Hell—just Hell. And you're a good woman."

Elizabeth was looking down. She could not bear his face.

"And would you say I was a truthful woman?" she said. "If I were to tell you the truth, would you believe me, David?"

"Yes," said David at once. "Yes, I'd believe you. If you told me anything at all you'd tell me the truth. Why shouldn't I believe you?"

"Because the truth is very unbelievable," said Elizabeth.

David lifted his head and looked at her.

"Oh, you'll not lie," he said.

"Thank you," said Elizabeth. After a moment's pause, she went on.

"Will you sit down, David? I don't think I can speak if you walk up and down like that. It's not very easy to speak."

He sat down in a big chair, that stood with its back to the window.

"David," she said, "when we were in Switzerland, you asked me how I had put you to sleep. You asked me if I had hypnotised you. I said, No. I want to know if you believed me?"

"I don't know what I believed," said David wearily. The question appeared to him to be entirely irrelevant and unimportant.

"When you hypnotise a person, you are producing an illusion," said Elizabeth. "The effect of what I did was to destroy one. But whatever I did, when you asked me to stop doing it, I stopped. You do believe that?"

"Yes—I believe that."

"I stopped at once—definitely. You must please believe that. Presently you will see why I say this."

All the time she had been standing quietly by the mantelpiece. Now she came across and kneeled down beside David's chair. She laid her hands one above the other upon the broad arm, and she looked, not at David at all, but at her own hands. It was the penitent's attitude, but David Blake, looking at her, found nothing of the penitent's expression. The light shone full upon her face. There was a look upon it that startled him. Her face was white and still. The look that riveted David's attention was a look of remoteness—passionless remoteness—and over all a sort of patience.

Elizabeth looked down at her strong folded hands, and began to speak in a quiet, gentle voice. The sapphire in her ring caught the light.

"David, just now you asked me why I married you. You never asked me that before. I am going to tell you now. I married you because I loved you very much. I thought I could help, and I loved you. That is why I married you. You won't speak, please, till I have done. It isn't easy."

She drew a long, steady breath and went on.

"I knew you didn't love me, you loved Mary. It wasn't good for you. I knew that you would never love me. I was—content—with friendship. You gave me friendship. Then we came home. And you stopped loving Mary. I was very thankful—for you—not for myself."

She stopped for a moment. David was looking at her. Her words fell on his heart, word after word, like scalding tears. So she had loved him—it only needed that. Why did she tell him now when it was all too late—hideously too late?

Elizabeth went on.

"Do you remember, when we had been home a week, you dreamed your dream? Your old dream—you told me of it, one evening—but I knew already—"

"Knew?"

"No, don't speak. I can't go on if you speak. I knew because when you dreamed your dream you came to me."

She bent lower over her hands. Her breathing quickened. She scarcely heard David's startled exclamation. She must say it—and it was so hard. Her heart beat so—it was so hard to steady her voice.

"You came into my room. It was late. The window was open, and the wind was blowing in. The moon was going down. I was standing by the window in my night-dress—and you spoke. You said, 'Turn round, and let me see your face.' Then I turned round and you came to me and touched me. You touched me and you spoke, and then you went away. And the next night you came again. You were in your dream, and in your dream you loved me. We talked. I said, 'Who am I?' and you said, 'You are the Woman of my Dream,' and you kissed me, and then you went away. But the third night—the third night—I woke up—in the dark—and you were there."

After that first start, David sat rigid and watched her face. He saw her lips quiver—the patience of her face break into pain. He knew the effort with which she spoke.

"You came every night—for a fortnight. I used to think you would wake—but you never did. You went away before the dawn—always. You never waked—you never remembered. In your dream you loved me—you loved me very much. In the daytime you didn't love me at all. I got to feel I couldn't bear it. I went away to Agneta, and there I thought it all out. I knew what I had to do. I think I had really known all along. But I was shirking. That's why it hurt so much. If you shirk, you always get hurt."

Elizabeth paused for a moment. She was looking at the blue of her ring. It shone. There was a little star in the heart of it.

"It's very difficult to explain," she said. "I suppose you would say I prayed. Do you remember asking me, if you had slept because I saw you in the Divine Consciousness? That's the nearest I can get to explaining. I tried to see the whole thing—us—the Dream—in the Divine Consciousness, and you stopped dreaming. I knew you would. You never came any more. That's all."

Elizabeth stopped speaking. She moved as if to rise, but David's hand fell suddenly upon both of hers, and rested there with a hard, heavy pressure.

He said her name, "Elizabeth!" and then again, "Elizabeth!" His voice had a bewildered sound.

Elizabeth lifted her eyes and looked at him. His face was working, twitching, his eyes strained as if to see something beyond the line of vision. He looked past Elizabeth as he had done in his dream. All at once he spoke in a whisper.

"I remembered, it's gone again—but I remembered."

"The dream?"

"No, not the dream. I don't know—it's gone. It was a name—your name—but it's gone again."

"My name?"

"Yes—it's gone."

"It doesn't matter, David."

Elizabeth had begun to tremble, and all at once he became aware of it.

"Why do you tremble?"

Elizabeth was at the end of her strength. She had done what she had to do. If he would let her go—

"David, let me go," she said, only just above her breath.

Instead, he put out his other hand and touched her on the breast. It was like the Dream. But they were not in the Dream any more. They were awake.

David leaned slowly forward, and Elizabeth could not turn away her eyes. They looked at each other, and the thing that had happened before came upon them again. A momentary flash—memory—revelation—truth. The moment passed. This time it left behind it, not darkness, but light. They were in the light, because love is of the light.

David put his arms about Elizabeth

"Mine!" he said.

THE END